STREET CHIĆ

A NOVEL BY

ANTHONY WHYTE

WHERE
HIP HOP
LITERATURE
BEGINS...

AUGUSTUS
PUBLISHING

© 2010 Augustus Publishing, Inc.
ISBN: 9780982541500

Novel by Anthony Whyte
Edited by Clarence Haynes
Creative Direction by Jason Claiborne

Augustus Publishing paperback June 2010
www.augustuspublishing.com

77107

Who you be?

Met this two headed whore in midtown
For skins, paid price, strapped up, tore it down
One head on my jewels, the other sucking
Working below stress, she wanted more
I'm wisdom, mention me next time.
"He who knows and knows he knows not;
He is simple— teach him."

I dismissed her come on as yap.
Others left chains and rings for less
Diamonds and pearls served rich men
"Shut your gap. Knowledge is power."
Was this trapping of my education?
"He who knows not and knows not
He knows not; he is a fool— shun him."

"At thirty, man suspects himself a fool;
Knows it at forty and reforms his plan;
At fifty chides his infamous delay,
Pushes his prudent purpose to resolve;
In all the magnanimity of thought
Resolves; and re-resolves; then dies the same."
I laid Edward Young, Night Thoughts on her
"He who knows and knows not he knows;
He is asleep— wake him."

Walking proudly, left a tip on her stand
Lost in the trap, she hurled what I'd given
Failing to understand, calling my offering
Nothing more than chump change
Accusing me of bringing false blessing
"He who knows and knows he knows;
He is wise— follow him."

Prologue

Claire smiled when she saw the way the swarm of police scrambled for cover. Dodging and ducking from the tremendous firepower coming from the shotguns in her possession. She fired again and again from her perch in the iron-sealed old abandoned warehouse. Claire felt power building in her mind. The same power she felt when she was running the park. She thought she had lost it. Watching her adversaries retreat confirmed what she felt. Claire never wanted to ever relinquish that feeling. She smirked, nodding and waiting. A stretch of calm followed the barrage. The police moved into strategic position, but were unable to completely surround the entire building. Parts of it had disappeared below ground.

The police were tactically retreating with complete realization that shots were coming from only one side of the warehouse. Realizing that the girls were outnumbered and outgunned, the police opened fire and unleashed heavy artillery. The loud sounds of explosion crashed into what had been the silence of the uneasy, but temporary cease-fire. Squads of trained police teams moved in on the warehouse, firing powerful caliber weapons. The resulting explosions spread around the girls like wildfire. They could see that the sun was beginning to set.

"A fine pickle we're in, big sis," Candace said, loading her weapons.

"Are you giving me the sad song, Candy?" Claire asked with sarcasm. She watched Candace clutching the weapons. "How's it?" she asked.

"We're running out of ammo," Candace answered.

"I hear you, Candy," Claire said.

"I'd be damn if I'm gonna be cooped up in anybody's prison, big sis," Candace said.

"Me too, Candy, me too," Claire agreed.

"I'm not afraid as long as you're with me, big sis. I know Mimmy will be sad that we went out like this," Candace said.

"People got do what they got to if they want to make it. There is no right or wrong way, Candy."

"Oh man, what a nice day to go out, huh big sis...?"

"Candy, it's time," Claire said, looking at the trap door.

Candace scurried over to it and attached the explosive device to the latch on the door. She grabbed an M203grenade launcher and fired a grenade through the window. The concussion ammunition landed in the center of the police squad moving forward. They quickly fell back, racing behind cover and returning fire. Bullets crashed through the warehouse with deadly accuracy. One hit the explosive device on the lock inside the abandoned building, causing a major explosion. Flames

and debris were hurled everywhere.

"Take cover, take cover!" squad leaders sounded off.

There were simultaneous explosions. Newsmen and camera crews jumped inside their news vans. Not far off, the situation was being closely followed by the occupants of a parked black sedan. Quietly observing the scene, Melanie, the only female of the three people occupying the car, shook her head. Pauli, the driver and right-hand man to his underboss, Goldie, made up the observing trio.

"Some friend you are. If those two were in there, then they gotta be deep sixed now. C'mon, let's get the fuck outta here," Goldie said.

"Ya right, nobody not even my girls could've survived that. And I love my girls. Now I gotta go buy something nice for their funeral," Melanie said. Both men turn to look at her seated next to Goldie in the backseat of the Bentley. "Shame, shame, shame," she continued. "They had so much talent, them two," she continued, pulling out a handkerchief and dabbing her eyes. "Too bad..."

"Hey Goldie, let's go find us a spot with some nice peppers and sausage," Pauli said.

"That's a good idea, Pauli," Goldie said. "Get me the fuck outta here."

"I know the perfect spot," Melanie said between tears.

They drove off leaving while the tactical squads were arriving. The police rushed into the destroyed warehouse and began searching through the rubbles. Shoulder to shoulder the units of the Miami Police and members of the FBI searched the destroyed warehouse. Their eyes were peeled for any evidence of the girls' body parts. Nothing was found. The police assumed that they had to have been killed. Their bodies were totally demolished in the explosion.

"I'm sorry, there's no one or nothing in here," the lieutenant said.

"Nothing...?" The captain echoed in disbelief.

"So far sir, no bodies, nothing... It's like they vanished in thin air. There's a canine unit on the way. We'll get the dogs in there, but so far nothing..."

"Good," the captain said in disgust.

He glanced around and walked away shaking his head. Seemingly caught up in sisters' demise, Lt. Cooksey stared at detective Street.

"Ha, ha, they deserve whatever they got," Lt. Cooksey said, laughing triumphantly.

Detective Street sat on the hood of the police cruiser watching him. She closed her eyes and whispered a silent prayer for the two sisters.

CHAPTER 1

Sheryl Street sat in a rental car staring through dark shades at the crowd of people entering Ortiz funeral home next to Fort Tryon Park, uptown Broadway. Feelings of whether what she had done to bring her this day was right or wrong ran amok in her troubled mind. Through her torment she saw them gossiping. Most of them she knew, they were from her old neighborhood at 179th Street and St. Nicholas Av.

Emotions were being displayed on the sleeves of everyone who was in the place. She could see the tear-stained faces even though their eyes were hidden by designers' shades. Sheryl didn't know if she wanted to deal with facing them, but she knew she had to attend.

A few more minutes went by and Sheryl took a couple of deep breaths. After adjusting her makeup, she got out of the car. Slamming the door shut, she turned and checked her appearance through the window. Her confidence was jarred and she slowly walked across the street. She was on her way to pay respect to the memory of Candace and Claire Osorio, her adopted sisters.

However, instead of showering her with hugs and greetings, mourners outfitted in black were waiting to rip her to shreds. Their deadly looks met her every shaky step. A bevy of mourners and character assassinators outfitted in distress drabs, pointed fingers while staring her down.

Digging her three-inch heels, black patent leather pumps into the floor, Sheryl held her head high without returning their threatening glares. She could feel the angry stares penetrating through the clothes that she wore. It didn't help that she had to keep adjusting her top because her thirty four C's were threatening to pop out. The outfit felt a little snug for any wake, especially this one, but it was all she had brought with her.

"That chica really looks chic," a mourner said.

Street glanced to see the face and caught a nasty snare from a young girl on the arms of her boyfriend. They snickered and rudely pointed their fingers at her.

"Yeah that's the cop that cause all this," the boyfriend scoffed.

Clothes weren't her only undoing. A change of mind could be costlier. She struggled with the decision she had made to attend. Sheryl did not plan on being at the wake, but changed her mind at the last minute. Entering Ortiz funeral home she immediately heard the dissent and started regretting her decision.

"She got some nerves!"

"That skank, that whore, she deserves a beat down!"

The voices of angry relatives and friends rang in her head, and Sheryl glanced at the door, wanting so badly to change her mind. Maybe she could go outside and explain her side of the story. Tell family and friends who no longer wanted to speak to her about all the pain raging inside of her. She felt like running away from it all, but Sheryl had to face up. There was a force stronger than any she could resist and it swept her in through the doors, and passed the angry rants behind mean stares greeting her.

Inside the small hall was set up like the inside of a small church. There were rows of benches on either side. Sheryl's presence caused tension to crackle like electricity in a lightning storm. Holding her breath, Sheryl Street stood in the eye of the controversy and felt her stomach muscles tightening.

Open chatter dogged her every move. She glanced without staring back and bit her lips. She released a heavy sigh while holding on to her emotions. Sheryl felt like breaking down and crying while making her way through the throngs of mourners. They turned their heads in the direction of the altar when she got close.

On top of the altar, two red urns filled with ashes sat on a stand filled surrounded by burning candles. The urns contained the remnants of her enigmatic adopted sisters Candace and Claire Osorio. Sheryl stared for a beat when she saw the photos on the wall behind.

Her tears flowed easily. She cried looking at video footage of the sisters playing basketball. Sheryl's conscience fell on her like a ton of bricks. She was directly involved in their deaths. Sheryl felt sorry for having come back. Still she had to face Mimmy, the woman who had raised all three of them. There were women here who used to greet her with hugs, now openly scoffed at her.

"Murdering cop, she really got some nerve showing her face round here after killing her own sisters," one woman in the tightest black dress said.

"But they weren't no flesh and blood," another noted.

"Mimmy raised them all didn't she?"

"Boy, Mimmy's coming soon. She's bound to kick that tight-butt bitch outta here," another suggested.

Their men stealing sips of liquor from a flask, stared at her backside, accentuated in a tight, dark Armani pantsuit. Lecherous stares from men whose wives and girlfriends despised her, greeted Sheryl with guarded pleasantries.

"I know you had to do what you had to do," one older man said, letting his eyes rove over her body before continuing. "Especially with you being the law and all," he smiled tastelessly, leering at her breasts.

Sheryl Street eyed him uneasily, pursing her lips while assuaging the urge she felt to deck him. She managed to hold back the impulse and nodded politely. Others in the crowded church grimaced walking by Street. They looked her up and down, cutting their eyes when they realized who she was. Sheryl walked down an aisle that appeared longer because of the tension. She wanted to pay her respects, but felt thick walls of resentment slowly closing in on her.

While waiting on a queue to get a closer look at pictures of the Osorio sisters, open whispers spilled around her. Sheryl felt sympathy for what she overheard in her quietness. She stared at the pictures of the girls. Closing her eyes and saying a silent prayer, Sheryl became caught up in a moment. It transferred her back to the time she first met Mimmy and her daughters. Sheryl was ten years old.

She had been living in an immigrant neighborhood in Opa Locka, on the outskirts of Miami, with her mother, Carmen, a Cuban immigrant. Her mother's boyfriend, Gilbert, would visit frequently and sometimes stay over. He was Haitian. Carmen was dependent on prescription drugs for her survival due to a bipolar condition. Often her mother would visit the local clinic and return at the end of the day with her prescriptions. One such day, Sheryl bade her mother goodbye and left for school. She knew her mother would be at the clinic all day and wouldn't be back until later that day.

That evening Sheryl waited patiently for her mother to come back from the clinic. She had hurried home from school and had not eaten. It was almost ten in the evening and her mother wasn't around. The following morning Sheryl awoke in a frantic mess. She had been unable to sleep very well through the night, and had forgotten to eat.

Even thought she was hungry and tired, Sheryl dragged herself to school. She raced home with anticipation beating in her heart. That evening Sheryl went to bed feeling depressed. The next day she still had not heard from her mother, and she still had not returned from the health clinic. After couple more days with no words or messages, Sheryl felt that her mother would never come back.

Gilbert eventually came by and she quizzed him about her mother's whereabouts. He provided her with no real answers. He was upset that she had been his girlfriend and had left without telling him, but he was irritated that he had to stay with her daughter. Gilbert guessed that she was at a friend's home, but Sheryl didn't seem to know exactly which relative's home she would be living in. Sheryl remembered her mother threatening that she may have to survive without her. Her mother may have really wanted to leave but Sheryl never took her seriously. Gilbert, from his guesses never took her words seriously either. Now they both realized it was more than idle chat.

Sheryl and Gilbert knew they were waiting in vain, but eventually developed a step-family relationship. Sheryl never knew her natural father. Gilbert told her he lived a short distance away from Opa Locka in the town of Little Havana. She stayed with her stepfather until, claiming he could no longer care for her. He brought Sheryl to live with Mimmy, his sister, in Washington Heights, New York City.

Sheryl was thirteen and puberty had already set in. Mimmy helped her a lot in understanding what she was going through in her maturing young girl cycle. In this respect, Gilbert was right to bring her to his sister. Mimmy was kind to her when she was most in need of it.

Without even a goodbye, Gilbert went back to Florida. Sheryl was left with Mimmy and tried to fit herself into a two bedroom apartment with two self-centered daughters and their drunken father. Candace and Claire were young and pretty and hated sharing their room with Sheryl. They got away with everything and often blamed anything that had gone wrong on the newcomer. The sisters always stuck together against her.

Sheryl replaced her dark shades and turned to walk back. She saw Mimmy coming toward her and stayed frozen in place. She had thought about what she would say and gone over the routine over and over in her head. Sheryl saw the older woman's heavy make-up. It did nothing to hide the pain and exhaustion wearing her down. Sheryl stopped to let her by but Mimmy held her ground and didn't budge. For what seemed like an eternity, the large woman's cold stare shot mercilessly through Sheryl like laser beams, tearing up her insides, and leaving her twisted in knots.

"I'm so sorry this had to happen..." Sheryl offered. Her emotions spilled over and her voice trailed.

After an eternity, Mimmy hobbled by without saying anything. Sheryl watched the familiar limp as Mimmy sauntered away. The woman who had raised her since she was ten and taught her to be the best at whatever she wanted to be turned her back on her. Sheryl watched Mimmy's gait. The robust woman had lost a step or two. It came from spending all those years being a nanny, and taking care of white kids on the upper west side. It was also that she had lost something special. Her two daughters had been her reason for living.

Mimmy was a Haitian immigrant who had married a man, Carlito Rafael Osorio from Santiago in the Dominican Republic. The family wasn't rich, but Mimmy did everything she could to provide for her daughters. Candace and Claire Osorio were really popular teens. They felt they had to keep up with the latest in fashion and be current with all the new trends. It was this craving that Mimmy sought to fill, but always seemed to be coming up a little short.

Neither sister tried hard in the classroom. They were average students who attended George Washington High School. Tall and athletically inclined, the sisters played sports and helped garnered many championship titles for the school. They excelled in basketball, baseball, and tracks for the school. In the Heights, the sisters were famous. Judging by the attendance in the church, the Osorio sisters were still revered and love.

Sheryl Street felt pangs of guilt streaming through her body as Mimmy Osorio knelt down, made the sign of the cross and quietly prayed. She still felt the same urge to run away like when she first walked in, but Sheryl also felt glued to her seat. She bowed her head, wordlessly begging God for absolution.

"There's no friend we have like Jesus and only He can grant you forgiveness..."

Sheryl looked up at the preacher with her mouth wide open. Suddenly her head hurt and she began to sweat profusely. Slowly, she got up and tiptoed to the exit. A series of nodding heads following her to the door.

"That's right! You better ease up outta here pig!"

"Yeah, that's it bitch, get to stepping!"

Their nasty comments chased her. She walked out to tiny droplets of rain. By the time she reached her car, it was coming down in buckets. Sheryl hastily jumped inside the comfort of the rented car and sat shaking her head. Slipping the key in the ignition, the engine hummed, drowning her sobbing. She heard honking and looked up to see what the clamoring was about.

Melanie Delgado, another childhood friend, had showed up with enough fanfare to stop any show. Cuban and connected to gangsters from all over the globe, Melanie was sitting in the black stretch. The dark tinted window came down. Melanie was screaming with a haunting greeting.

"Had ya fair-share, cop-bitch? Ya can't take it anymore, huh? No one wants ya ass around here anyhow. Ya know the way outta town bitch-cop...!"

Sheryl Street stared at Melanie and a group of well dressed men. Without saying anything in response, she slipped her shades on. Sheryl gunned the powerful engine and took off with nowhere special to go. She knew she had to get away.

Coming back to the city had proven a point. There was no further need to stay. But maybe there was one more thing she needed to do. She had wanted to talk to Mimmy. Her telephone calls had gone unanswered and she had never got a chance to say her piece. Now it didn't seem likely to happen. Mimmy was too bitter. It was time to go, clear her head and try another time.

She found herself going up the familiar steep hill. These were her old haunts. Sheryl guided the car through the neighborhood she knew all too well. She looked at Mimmy's apartment building. It was where all the kids from the neighborhood used to congregate on the steps. Sheryl remembered the last time when they all gathered at the steps.

"Yeah, here comes Orphan Annie," Melanie teased.

Sheryl's cheek smart from the jibe, but she held herself in check. Instead she countered with a question about school.

"I'm going to Florida for college. Where are you headed Melanie?"

"If I've gotta live in Florida, it won't be for no school, ya heard? After graduation I'm through with this school stuff. I'm gonna make me some money. It'll be all about the money for me," Melanie said.

"Melanie's right. School's helped me enough already. I think I've learned how to count my money," Candace smiled.

"I agree with them. You're wrong Orphan Annie," Claire

surmised. "But it's good that you're going to college in Florida. Maybe you might find a relative or someone for you."

That night, Sheryl had difficulty sleeping in her hotel room and couldn't wait for the morning. When it came, she hurried through showering. After slipping into the same dark skirt outfit, Sheryl spent a lot of time at the make-up stand trying to cover the dark circles around her eyes. She wanted to face Mimmy one more time. Stopping at a café for breakfast, Sheryl couldn't keep her mind off Mimmy. During her second cup of coffee, she read about the ordeal in a local daily newspaper.

Mourners gathered outside a funeral home in order to get a glimpse of the detective whose bullets caused the deaths of her adopted sisters. "I've cut all ties to my former adopted daughter, Sheryl Street, before she killed my babies..."' Mimmy Osorio, the woman who raised Sheryl and her sisters Candace and Claire Osorio, said after learning that her daughters were killed in a fiery stand-off with police in South Florida. The girls, both twenty-three years old, were accused of a wave of shoplifting and were being sought by the NYPD for the murders of key witnesses involved in the case against them. Detective Shirley Street headed a team of investigators that included members of the NYPD larceny squad and detectives from the Dade County in Miami. For over a year authorities had been searching for the sisters who grew up in Washington Heights and were local high school basketball and volleyball stars. Somewhere along the line their lives took a whirl into the land of crime. The deaths of the two women have left questions. Detective Street has known the victims since she was eight years old. The victims were...

Shaking her head, Sheryl couldn't read anymore. She left the tearstained daily on the breakfast table. Sheryl put on her shades and headed to the parking lot. She turned the radio on and quickly changed the station from a newscast. The light, melodic jazz calmed her nerves and cleared the frown she wore.

Sheryl gazed unexcitedly out the window, driving back across the George Washington and riding along 178th Street. Approaching the old neighborhood, she eased her foot up off the gas pedal. Her mind raced to recollect all the memories that quickly fell back into place.

Mimmy had tried to provide the best for all the girls, and was mostly out of the home. She worked as a nurse's aide in a Jewish hospital in Staten Island. Mimmy used to travel back and forth from Staten Island to Manhattan to give her daughters the best. They were her only children and even though the marriage ended in disaster. Her husband and father of her girls, walked out with a younger woman. Mimmy worked hard to help the girls forget him. She went out of her way for the young Candace and Claire.

They would get anything they wanted and Mimmy always obliged. A month after Sheryl was residing with them they wanted a new volleyball set for all their friends to play with at the park. The sisters were fourteen and hung out with older friends in front of the building. Mimmy clearly didn't like their friends but she went out of her way to run to the store and get them the set.

"I told you she..." Candace started, but Claire cut her off.

"But Mimmy, you said you were gonna..."

As soon as Claire started, Mimmy reached into her bag and pulled out a ball. The girls jumped and screamed, clearly excited by the sight of the volleyball and net. Jacque was a good friend and would be in the midst of everything, came running from next door.

"Wha' happened?"

"Oh she got it, the whole set," Claire cheered.

"Mimmy, you're the best," said both girls in unison and Jacque started rejoicing with them.

"Now, we could go to the park, huh Mimmy?" Candace asked.

"You can. Please be careful. And please come back before it gets too dark."

"Let me go with y'all. Y'all two gonna need some protection,"

Jacque said.

"Not from no sissy..." Claire said.

"C'mon girls, play nice..." Mimmy said.

"It's okay Mimmy, Jacque can handle himself," Jacque said, his hands on his hips.

"You need to stop!" Candace said, waving her hand.

"You can play with orphaned Annie over there," said Claire, pointing at Sheryl.

"Since our uncle left, she's been acting funny you know? Retarded..."

They both giggled and ran off. Mimmy called out after them.

"Claire, Candace, listen up both of you; I spent my last dollar buying that damn ball. I don't wanna hear about y'all losing it. Y'all understand?"

"Yes Mimmy," the sisters responded in unison.

"Lord, I have spoiled them rotten. What can I say, they're mine," Mimmy smiled. "Sheryl, please, you and Jacque follow my girls and watch out for them. Make sure nothing happens to them. I'm gonna see what's inside the fridge for dinner."

Jacque stared at Sheryl and they both nodded. Candace and Claire always have their way. They hurried to play with their new volleyball.

"We know the perfect spot," Candace said, pointing to an area in the park with trees that had low hanging branches.

Claire was the oldest by two years and the leader of the pack.

Candace always stuck with her sister through thick and thin. They were tall and beautiful and not only went everywhere together, but the sisters also did everything together.

When they arrived at River Bank Park, it was crowded. A group of young white kids picnicking grudgingly watched Claire and Candace setting up the volleyball net. Snickers and sneers were thrown in the players' direction. Sheryl and Jacque played on one side while Claire and Candace teamed up. Sheryl and Jacque played hard but the sisters were very tall at an early age, agile and athletic.

The games got more intense and Jacque struck first, sending the ball out of bounds one too many times in the midst of the picnickers. The girls chased the ball another time when Candace spiked it too hard. One of the kids standing around grabbed the ball and threw it in the direction of another member of the group.

"Give it back!" Claire demanded, walking toward the group.

"Why y'all want to mess around?" Candace asked excitedly.

"Hold up, Candace. Wait a minute. You know your temper, girl?" Jacque was shouting running after the girls as he and Sheryl followed, trying to keep the peace.

"Yeah, and if I don't, what?" the boy holding the ball replied and tossed the ball to another boy when Claire took a few steps closer.

She watched the ball being tossed around in the group. The routine continued for five minutes. They were all tired of waiting for the ball to be returned.

"Give me my ball or else..." She preened, strutted, and started her head-wagging routine.

"Or else what...? What're you gonna do?"

Claire reached for her ball and one of the guys shoved her. She made another attempt. This time he shoved her so hard, she fell backwards and hit her head. Jacque rushed to her help her.

"Jacque is she alright?" shouted Sheryl.

Jacque knelt next to the fallen and unconscious Claire. He checked her pulse as if he was a paramedic then shot a mean stare, batting his eyes at the guy who had pushed Claire.

"You mean, lily, white bully. I oughta..."

"Listen you lil' black fag, I'll kick your teeth in if you so much as look this way again. Why don't you and your girlfriends go on your side of the park...?"

"Hey, what'd do to my sister?" shouted Candace.

"I done told y'all, you are not welcome on this side."

The group laughed as Candace and Jacque tried their best to resuscitate Claire. It seemed like an eternity. Candace shook with fear but bravely gave her sister mouth-to-mouth, trying to revive Claire. It was a procedure she had learned in swimming class. Candace gently shook her sister. The cobwebs seemed to clear from Claire's dazed mind. Close to tears, she and Jacque were able to finally help Claire to her feet.

"Claire, Claire..."

"Who got the ball?" asked Claire.

"Forget about the ball, are you..." Jacque started.

"Forget it? No way, Mimmy told us not to lose that ball," Claire said, jumping up and brushing herself off. "I'm not leaving without our ball," she said, blinking rapidly and shaking her head.

"Oh girl, why don't you just forget that damn ball," offered Jacque, dragging Claire back from the picnickers.

"Jacque you're such a sissy..."

"Shoot, I'd rather be a live sissy than a dead brave boy."

"Hold up, why we walking away? We ain't leaving without my damn volleyball," Claire said, brushing off Jacque.

"He got our ball," Candace firmly said, pointing to the white teen.

He was smiling, proudly holding the ball. They walked over to where the group of kids stood sunning and guffawing.

"Uh oh, here they come again..." one of them said.

"They must want some more," another laughed.

"Give me back my fucking ball," Claire yelled.

"Ooh... Or what...?"

"She gonna break your heart with them tears..."

The group broke out in laughter.

"I'm gonna ask you for the last time..."

"Or what...?"

"She's gonna blow your dick... Ha, ha, ha..."

"Yeah bitch, do this..." the boy taunted.

They were laughing so hard, the kid with the ball didn't see Claire swing. The blow caught him in the soft of his throat, catching the boy off guard. He staggered, choking.

"Shit, th-th-this bitch just hi-hit me..." he said coughing up blood. He wiped the red liquid trickling from his mouth.

There was no chance for a recovery. Claire was on him, hitting him hard with another left, and a right. Her Reeboks landed in his groin, leaving him doubled over.

"Whoever wanna clown c'mon step up." Claire said, recovering the ball.

She tossed it to Jacque. Candace moved in behind her while Jacque cowered next to Sheryl.

"It wasn't me..." a kid screamed when Claire rushed him.

"Kick his ass Claire! Who they think they is anyhow...?" Jacque hollered, puffing up his chest.

"I wasn't down with it from the jump," one said.

"It was not my idea... He did it," another said pointing at the teen spitting blood.

Claire stared at the teen cringing with his bloodied lips and felt something surging through her veins. She was the victor and he was the vanquished. This thought caused a surge of power to rush through her frame. It made her feel like she had super powers. Claire smiled and walked away.

"Damn girl, you punched his ass out. He was so dazed his homey had to help him out. What do you have in those fist of yours, girlfriend?" Jacque snickered.

CHAPTER 2

The girls were very close and grew even closer the older they got. Popular and admired, Claire and Candace Osorio hung together so tightly that nearly everyone thought they were twin sisters. Claire was the older by two years to the baby-faced Candace. Despite being in different classes, the girls were always seen together in school. Whether they were hanging in the halls or playing basketball, they were with each other constantly. They never seemed bored with each other's company.

Not only were they the most athletic pair on the school's varsity teams, but they were the tallest and the best players. From volleyball to basketball and baseball, it didn't matter. The Osorio sisters were winners at their games.

Best friend and neighbor, Jacque was always with them. He was tall but lacked real athletic skills unless dancing fit the category. Jacque guided them and watched over them like a trained Chihuahua, with a loud bark that drew plenty attention. It was his way. Then they met Melanie, a Cuban girl. She was much older and experienced in every aspect of living. She quickly became the girls influence, especially Candace. Jacque was a member of the marching band and he was Cuban. Melanie was not athletic— simply beautiful, cunning, saucy and vivacious. From the very jump, everyone could tell she carried a Latina fire that burned anyone she didn't like within her vicinity.

It was also known to everyone that she would go for whatever. Whether straight or bi, Melanie was down to do whatever it took to get her way. The first time Jacque encountered Melanie was a day never to be forgotten. She had her eyes on the athletically built sisters but it was clear, Jacque was smitten.

Melanie was walking with the sisters. Jacque saw them in their sexy outfits and walked over. The sisters always looked really good but Melanie was ravishing.

"Are you on detention, Jacque?" Candace asked.

"No, why...?"

"You don't even come to school enough. And when you do come, you overstay your day? Oh, you're trying to make up for lost time?" Candace cackled and Claire laughed.

"Everybody wants to be a comedian, huh?" Jacque deadpanned.

He turned to Melanie standing next to them. Jacque ogled every inch of her curves. When he was satisfied, he turned to Sean, nodding. They struck a high five and posed for a beat. Jacque turned to Melanie with his pearly whites on display.

"Hi, I'm Jacque. I know you're Melanie. Fuck what they say about you, you're beautiful, girl," he announced in his most social voice.

"Are you trying to push-up on our friend?" Claire teased.

"Melanie, Jacque has never had a girlfriend and if you give him some he won't know how to act..." Candace started as Jacque stare shot to the roof. Rolling his eyes, he stomped his Nike in the hall.

"Get out! You mean he's a virgin?" Melanie shouted too loud. "Why don't you give him some na-na?" she whispered to Candace.

"She can't stand mustaches, especially down there..." Claire remarked. "And Jacque not only wears a mustache, but he has the whole goatee look going on," Claire laughed.

"Too sensitive down there, huh...?" Melanie laughed.

The conversation brought nosy schoolmates. Jacque, his hands on his hips, stood glowering at the sisters and Melanie.

"It's my pleasure to meet you too, bitches," Jacque said after minutes of steaming.

"Boy, you better watch your mouth," Melanie responded with a smile. "You behave and I might let you have some," she laughed.

"See you later, lover. We'll hangout later after practice. I'll put in a word for you if you come to class," Candace smiled.

"But Mimmy is expecting us to be home right after—" Sheryl started but Candace interrupted.

"We do what we wanna do Orphan Annie, and don't you forget that!" Claire said.

"Candy, if you need someone else to go downtown, then I'll shave for you, Candy baby," Rick interjected.

"Hey dip-shit, her name isn't Candy. So you can go ahead with all that yang, and count yourself out of the running to get anything from my sister. I'm the only one who calls her Candy. Understand stupid?" Claire said.

"We should be heading home now. Mimmy is expecting..."

"Stop worrying so much Orphan Annie. As far as Mimmy knows, we'll be late cause we were at track practice," Claire said.

"And you better not say anything else, or else," Candace chimed in.

"Y'all got this orphan chica in check," Melanie snickered.

They laughed and walked away. Jacque and Sean were left shaking their heads. When Jacque realized all eyes were on him, he smiled and waved. He and Sean watched their backfields in motion. The three girls sashayed out of view. Jacque smiled that day watching Candace pulling Melanie away. He secretly decided that Melanie would be the one he was going to lose his virginity to.

After their first encounter, Jacque treated Melanie really special and quickly became her best friend forever. Candace, who used to be his special interest, quickly became a past fling. She hadn't lost in anything but realized that she was an also ran, his backup plan.

"Ooh whew!" he whistled as Sean, his male best friend, came running over to him.

"Jacque, what's up, son?"

"This damn school still pissing me the fuck off..." Jacque said.

"You finished with detention?"

"I'm out here, right?"

"Claire and Candace are looking real good?"

"But did you see that Melanie Vasquez who was with them. She's got a walk to make a gay man straight. She's mine."

"What about Candace?" Sean asked.

"Candace will always be my soul-mate," Jacque laughed.

Over the next couple weeks, Candace watched in dismay as Claire went out of her way to hook up Jacque and Melanie. They made a bet that Jacque wanted to lose his virginity to Melanie instead of Candace. She didn't believe he would, but went along with the program. Claire planned to set them up when they went to the annual school dance.

Jacque was always well dressed. Like a male model, his tall wispy but muscular frame was sporting a purple suit. He spent most of the night chatting and laughing with Melanie. Later on, he was seen leaving the party with the giggling Melanie on his arm. She took him to her place. He and Melanie were upstairs in her bedroom kissing when the phone rang. Melanie pulled away from his embrace to get the phone.

"Do you have to take that call?" he asked Melanie.

"Yes," she laughed pulling her top off. "It's for ya ass..."

Jacque looked at her strangely, and reluctantly took the phone.

"Yes...?"

"That's it nigga, ya ain't never getting any of this ass. Ya hear boy..."

The voice was loud and Jacque stared at the phone with surprise all over his face. It was Candace. He could hear Claire laughing in the background.

"You fucking fag! You better enjoy that Cuban pussy because you ain't getting any of this, ever. You can ask your man, Sean, and he'll tell you what it feels like to fuck Claire and Candace Osorio. Bye Jacque!"

He put the phone down and stared with the look of a lovelorn putz at the sexy Melanie and tried to smile. She let out a big laugh and pushed his face into the cleavage of her breast. Jacque drooled. Things happened fast and before he knew it, Jacque was putting on his jacket and being escorted out the door.

Waiting for him when he reached outside Melanie's apartment were Candace, Claire and Sean. They were all smiles.

CHAPTER 3

Mimmy tried to give her daughters all they wanted. This tendency of fulfilling their every need caused the girls to expect others around them to do the same. Victims would often be seduced and deceived by the spoiled rotten Osorio sisters. The blame could clearly have rested on the shoulders of their hardworking mother, stirred by the conniving talents of Melanie.

Sadistically they seemed to enjoy destroying anything they couldn't have after taking all that was given. They did this equally well and with no remorse. Sheryl knew it first hand when they started on her. Candace and Claire constantly riled her about her past and Mimmy did nothing to put it to rest. Sometimes she even encouraged it.

"Hey, you better get tough skin if their silly words are gonna bother you," Mimmy said.

Sheryl had just been told for the umpteenth time that she was an orphan. The joke had gotten old to her but not apparently to Mimmy. Jacque, who seemed to be always visiting, was there and tried to speak on her behalf.

"There are penalties for everything you do and they'll get theirs in the end," Jacque said.

He was there trying to see Candace. After his sexual episode with Melanie, Candace was always too tired to speak to him. Jacque came around looking for her and heard both her and Claire clowning. Mimmy didn't intervene.

"Jacque why are you all up in the family's biz?" asked Candace.

"Why have you been avoiding me?" he asked turning the tables.

"You're asking question like you have warrants or sump'n," Candace said.

"You haven't been returning my calls. What's up, Candace?"

"Where your mouth been?" she asked.

"On my face..."

"Are you sure?" Candace laughed.

"What's really good?"

"Last week, I made a bet and lost," she answered dryly.

"And...?"

"I thought I knew the person and couldn't lose. I thought

wrong, Jacque. Claire won."

"Claire...? Oh she never plays fair."

"She did this time."

"What was the bet about?"

"I bet her that you wouldn't fuck Melanie..."

Jacque opened his mouth but no answer came. Finally he released a heavy sigh.

"That's a fucked up thing to do but I never did anything. I'm still a virgin," he breathed. "Believe in me Candace..."

His voice trailed off, and he could no longer continue the lie when he saw the evil look on her face. It made him lightheaded. Candace and Claire started hanging with Melanie and her father, a self proclaimed Cuban refugee living in Washington Heights. Papa was a drunk who hung out at the bodega on the corner, and tried to tell his life story for a Budweiser to anyone. Candace and Claire were popular and very playful.

Whenever they went out, Mimmy always encouraged Sheryl to accompany the sisters to make sure they didn't get out of hand. Slowly with the help of Melanie and her father, the girls launched a life of crime. Then they underestimated what they were up against once store owners started letting them slide. It started out with Sheryl unwittingly following the sisters and Melanie into a boutique called Le Chic.

"Let's check out this place," suggested Melanie, winking.

Melanie, Candace and Claire planned on stealing but conveniently forgot to tell Sheryl. They moved cautiously into position and noticed that security was in the back.

"That just makes our getaway so much easier," Candace said.

Melanie found a pair of jeans and Candace found two tops. She checked the sizes. They were perfect. She stashed them in Sheryl's backpack. They were about to leave the store, and a security guard swooped down, blocking their exit. He brought them back into the store and wouldn't let them go until after Sheryl spent all the money she had on the stolen items. The store owner knew Melanie's father and notified him. Papa was there an hour later, half drunk and talking plenty trash.

Sheryl was sick to her stomach from embarrassment. Candace was scared that Papa would report the incident to Mimmy. Claire tried to diffuse the situation. Claire's mind was working fast.

"Hey Papa," she greeted the old man. "You know us better..." Claire started.

"Back home in my country, I'd whip yer ass until y'all were sore. But in this country you can get away with anything, if you know the way..."

"What?" the girls answered at the same time.

"Are you gonna report us?" Claire asked. They watched him, unsure.

"Huh? What? The system doesn't help," responded Papa.

Silence followed. Papa took a swallow of some brown liquor and scratched his head as if thinking of their punishment. Then he let out a soft chuckle. The girls watched, perplexed by his behavior. He led them to a park bench and sat them down.

"Come have a seat and let's chat about the birds and the bees," Papa said.

They did as told and sat uncomfortable, waiting for his next move.

"Let me school you to the art of boosting before y'all end up in the slammer," he said with a drawl.

Melanie, Claire and Candace looked at each other then back to Papa. They watched Sheryl staring at them with a look of difference. She walked away, disappearing inside a McDonald's restaurant.

"Rule number one; know your territory. Ya gotta sniff out all the security systems. And be familiar with all the exits but always have at least two ways out and a back-up. Rule number two; be casual and always walk slowly to the merchandise. You don't want to arouse suspicions."

"It's that easy, huh?" Claire said.

"Only if you're confident in what you're doing, a well planned job is rarely fucked up" Papa answered.

"We're young, so what happens if security follows you around?" Candace asked.

"Yeah, like they always do..." Melanie joined in.

Papa was about to speak, but took a sip of brew instead, when he saw Sheryl's glare when she returned.

"I can't believe that you guys are sitting here listening to this after what you've just been through?" Sheryl lectured.

The sisters waved her off and no one paid her any attention to what she was saying.

"That leads us to the third rule. Always dress to kill. That makes the sales people less nervous and they think you've got dough."

"That's easy for you to say, but who's gonna believe we got money?" Claire asked.

"Tricks of the trade y'all can use in the future. Only use it if your heart is in it."

"What makes you think that we even wanna live like that?" Claire asked, cutting in.

"In my travels as a refugee, I've met a lot of good people and a lot of bad ones."

"And what...?" Claire asked.

"You two are fearless beauties, athletic and smart. With a little development you two can..."

"You think we have more heart than all these others..." Claire started.

"If you can remember not to disturb your elders when they talk, then the sky's the limit for you two. You mark my words."

"Papa, tell 'em about how ya met Sammy the Bull..." Melanie encouraged.

"Si, we once shared the same cell. I once saved his life, which reminds me that whenever you find that someone is trying to go against you, then that person must be eliminated... Do all you can do to rid yourselves of that kinda person," Papa said, and took a long sip of brown liquor. "Never get involved with this shit," he said, holding up the fifth of Brugal Rum. He drank some more. "Listen to Papa," he continued. "He knows."

"What do we owe you for this?" Claire asked.

"Stay true to Papa and promise never to steal from one another. Game's over when you start stealing from each other," Papa said, snapping his fingers.

"Papa, that's it? You tell me before never to kill a cop?" Melanie asked.

"That was when you were alone...now you got a team." Papa smiled and raised his bottle.

"Papa if we..." Claire started.

"You two haven't given me your promise yet," Papa said.

The girls looked speechlessly at each other. Claire raised her eyebrow and nodded to her younger sister. They turned and faced the drinking man. He seemed hardly able to handle the liquor. The smell, like his thick accent, was heavy on his breath when he opened his mouth.

"Well... What y'all gonna say?"

"You've got our word, Papa. We promise not to steal from each other," the girls chorused.

"And I'm talking about from the heart," he smiled and coughed.

"Can we go now?" Sheryl pleaded.

"Okay, then that's it. She's right. Ya gals better get going now." Papa led the girls to the train station.

"Papa, c'mon, I got some questions..." Candace said.

"That's it girls, classes finished. Get home safely and remember it is very important to never break your promise. Now stay in school."

"But you can't make any money doing that," Candace said.

"Yeah, but you'll be able to count the number of years you two will get if you follow that drunken old man's advice. Now please let's go," Sheryl deadpanned.

"You don't have to be soo bossy," Candace said.

"Ah man, she's just hating, 'cause she's an orphan," Claire added.

"You know I do have parents," Sheryl said.

"And they probably ran off because you're so mean," Claire said.

"I'll find them someday. And if I don't, then I really won't need them."

The girls walked quietly back to the home. Candace and Claire were thinking of their new game, boosting, while Sheryl was contemplating leaving New York for college.

CHAPTER 4

"When are we gonna do that...?"

Sheryl overheard Candace on the phone. Probably with Melanie, she thought. A couple weeks after the incident, Candace and Claire were still at it. Sheryl took a stance and went to Mimmy and told her the reason for spending all the money in one boutique. The sisters were in the bathroom playfully watching each other get dressed.

"Why Miss Claire, you look soo wonderful, big sis."

"I do thank you, Miss Candy. I'd say you're looking quite ravishing."

They laughed lightheartedly. Their tone changed to a more serious one as they continued to admire themselves.

"Really though, they ain't ready for this," Candace said, smacking her sister's naked ass.

"Show me what you're working with," Claire said.

It was then that Mimmy blasted through the bathroom door in a huff of fury.

"How dare y'all do that crazy shit in Washington Heights? I'm not raising any common thieves..."

"Mimmy, we weren't doing anything. It was Sheryl's fault..."

"Don't tell lies, girl. Melanie's father already spoke to me..."

"That ol' Orphan Annie bitch..."

"Go to your room, right now! You're both grounded," Mimmy thundered.

During the summer of 2004, the sisters gave Sheryl the hardest time of her young life. They told so many lies that Mimmy kept Sheryl on whole month of punishment. She stayed on Mimmy's bad side. Mimmy forbade her to leave the apartment.

Many a summer nights when Sheryl would rather be out, she was in the apartment. Resentment for her spilled over in the way Mimmy treated her. There were times she felt like running away. Sheryl wished for her mother. She wanted badly to see the woman who was now seven years removed from her life. During this time, she cried a lot. Sheryl made a pact to search for her mother and let her know about the misery her leaving had caused.

Claire and Candace were now freed of Sheryl's involvement. Along with Melanie, they embarked on a summer robbery spree. On a regular basis, they would be boosting, hanging out in clubs, and shoplifting. It got so hot that by the middle of summer, the police were also after Melanie. The police turned up the heat, and she had to flee NYC before the end of summer. It was rumored she was in Florida but no one knew for sure. If they did, they weren't telling. The Osorio sisters started their own crime crusade.

Toward the end of the summer, Sheryl Street happily moved back to Florida, vowing never to return. She had graduated from high school along with the sisters. Their plans were to move to Hollywood and become rich and famous actresses. In the meantime, Claire and Candace were busy establishing another career.

"All right, strap yourself in sis. Look-out Fifth Avenue, here comes the Osorio sisters."

It was early July and the shopping district was crowded. The stores were receiving fall merchandise and all were busy. Summer sales attracted so many shoppers that sales staffs and security were constantly hopping around. Candace and Claire joined the fracas. The shopping grid stretched out blocks and blocks along Fifth and Madison Avenues. They were charming and smiles but there was only one thing on their minds—boosting.

They checked the store security after waltzing into Armani. They sashayed in and out of Christian Dior, Gucci, and Valentino before finally hitting Dolce and Gabbana. The girls kept it moving from sales racks to sales rack while steering clear of the salespeople in Saks. They did an end to end sweep of Giorgio's, carefully inspecting merchandise. All the while they smiled, cataloging the security systems in their memory banks.

"Damn, it's crowded in all these stores," Claire observed. "I can't really operate like I want to."

"Let's head over to Saks," Candace suggested. "It might not be as crowded."

"Candy, I want those new Gucci boots today..." Claire started, but Candace interrupted her.

"We'll do Gucci in a minute, big sis."

Claire and Candace exited carrying large shopping bags. They walked into Gucci and headed for the leather to sample the couture.

"Good day ladies. May I be of some assistance?" a salesgirl greeted.

"No thanks," Candace smiled seductively.

"Very well... Enjoy your day at Gucci."

"Thank you," Claire said.

"Claire, check out those over there," Candace said.

"Let's get to the shoe department first," Claire said.

"No, let's hit that on our way out," Candace said.

She was looking at a pair of leather pants and carefully examining the security locks attached.

"Big sis, this is really hot," Candace said.

"Yeah Candy, they're very nice," Claire nonchalantly replied.

"Okay, I got it. Let's see what they got in the shoe department," Candace said, shaking her head. Claire followed wearing a smug smile.

Later at lunch, Claire and Candace laughed and talked about the adventure that quickly became their calling card. The girls auspiciously began their boosting career. The girls boasted about slipping by security systems. Their arms were filled with the days' loot as they made their way to the train station.

"Lunch was really great. I was so hungry," Candace said as they walked on to the platform.

"I want some new perfumes," Claire said.

"Let's go get them," Candace said.

Confident but playful, the girls walked past a few high-end boutiques and beaneries in search of the nearest perfume store.

CHAPTER 5

Sheryl left New York City to attend college in Florida. She wanted to be as far away as possible and nothing to do with the family that had partially raised her. Sheryl resumed living with her step dad, Gilbert, on a day by day basis.

The heckling from both sisters was enough to drive Sheryl crazy. Furthermore she didn't like the way they took advantage of Mimmy. It hurt her every time they lied to Mimmy and she had to help them with the covering up. Sheryl would do anything to get away from Candace and Claire. Including living with and caring for an alcoholic stepfather.

Although money was tight, Sheryl was able to transfer her credits and started as a junior at Florida A&M. Sheryl Street was looking to establish her independence. In so doing, the calls to her former caretaker, and unofficial adopted mother, Mimmy, grew less and less. Thoughts of her natural mother's whereabouts taunted her more and more. It was during this time that Sheryl became interested in law and order. The idea hit after she had watched a recruiting advertisement on early morning television.

"*...Further your career as an attorney while working as a police officer for Dade County...*"

Sheryl explored further. She found that the county would not only pick up the cost of her legal studies, but she would be paid once she joined the department. It was a no-brainer. Through the police department she would be able to track her mother's whereabouts easily. Sheryl found all the resources that could significantly change her life, and she couldn't wait to make the jump. The day came and her heart was almost jumping from her chest with excitement. When she went in, and put the uniform on, it was the most exhilarating feeling from a single move she could make.

During this time, Candace and Claire went about making their names boosting in New York. By daytime, they ran constant raids on the downtown shopping area and malls around the Tri-state area of Connecticut, New York and New Jersey. At nights they hung out at the most popular clubs for the rich and famous. The three girls seemed made for the work and did it to the best of their abilities. Through the people Jacque knew, they were able to hold sales on boosted items. Their appetite for stealing brought them money but the girls never seemed to have enough.

"What would we be doing if we weren't into this?" Candace asked.

"I don't know," Claire said, watching Candace toying with the rare sirloin in front of her.

"I want to be so rich, I could eat out at the best restaurants all the time," Candace said.

"Candy, I hate fucking rich people," Claire said.

"I'll do whatever I have to make a lot of money, big sis."

"Yeah...? Would you let a man fuck you, Candy?" Claire asked.

"You know I hate all men, big sis," Candace said. "They're motherfuckers."

"Listen sis, just because your father hurt you and..." Claire started and Candace immediately got up.

"Let's pay this tab and bounce. It's getting a little too sentimental around here," Candace said.

The girls revisited the scene of their Fifth Ave crimes at Elizabeth Arden's. Claire lifted the perfume she had been craving. Candace was busy distracting the salesgirls.

"Will that be all today, Miss?" the salesclerk asked, packing away the item. Not to be outdone, Candace jacked an expensive bottle of men's cologne. Claire paid for a small bottle of cologne and Candace stole a couple more bottles of fragrances right from under the salesclerk's nose. The girls walked out the store and joined the crowded sidewalk. They spotted the Prada store and decided to help themselves.

"Oh don't tell me you're going there," Candace said.

"I can't have too many Pradas," Claire quipped.

The girls sauntered inside, touching the merchandise. Their sexy, chic look reminded one of the salesgirls of runway models. She inquired.

"I'm sorry to intrude but I couldn't help but ask. Are you two models? I know I've seen your faces before...at a show, maybe...?"

"Maybe..." Candace answered.

"I know, the stars always sez maybe. I'll keep your secret." Convincing herself that the girls were super models, she smiled and walked away. Claire and Candace were left with a shopping bag and carte blanche to take as many items as they wanted into the dressing room.

Once inside, the sisters worked in unison. Moving rapidly but disciplined, they removed their clothing and Candace took care of the security tags from all the items except one. She cut the label and used a Sharpie to mark defect on the item.

Claire was busy removing tags on their clothing. They both slipped into the new duds and put the old ones in the bags. They placed the unaltered items on the top. The duo exited the dressing room in a hurry. Salesgirls tried engaging them by presenting to them some new suits. They disregarded her and were out of the store before she could recover.

In any one evening, Claire and Candace would hit several stores including Dolce and Gabbana, Coach, and Versace. Using several various wigs and makeup to disguise themselves, the girls stole several thousand dollars of merchandise. By the time the dust would settle, the girls were long gone in a taxi.

"I think those stores have seen us for a week," Candace said.

"You think...?" Claire chimed.

Having done a days work, the girls relaxed inside their Manhattan apartment. Claire poured herself and Candace, Gin and tonic.

"Make mine on the rocks," Candace said.

Claire swallowed the drink. She mixed another while Candace slipped out of her clothes and busied herself checking the bags. She found a leather skirt and held it against her hips.

"These will fit me nicely."

She wiggled her naked ass around the apartment. Then turned and strolled as if she was on a runway.

"Smile for the cameras..." Claire said, handing her a drink. "Damn you've gotta be the best booster I know. How did you get the locks off?"

"That's for me to know and you to find out. I see you with that heavy-duty bottle of Channel. Inquiring minds wanna know how you didn't get caught?" Candace laughed.

"See, there's this lil' sump'n called hypnosis," Claire answered with a wink. She picked out a cute silk blouse and pulled her top over her head. Topless, she massaged her perfect breast.

"I'll wear this without a bra," she smiled.

Candace put the drink to her head and swallowed. They fell back in the plush leather sofa, toasting.

"This is the life." Candace said raising her glass.

"Ah... the bliss," Claire said smiling.

They started unpacking their bounty for the day.

"I can't believe that store wanted two thousand for this jacket," Candace said.

"It was actually twenty-five hundred dollars, girl," Claire corrected.

"It's insane whatever the amount."

"Candy, you're not answering my question?"

"What was that?" Candace asked.

"Those sensors...? The ones you pulled off in Gucci today? Last week when we were in ah Saks, you did it. And you did that shit in Victoria's Secret last week too. Don't front. C'mon Candy, you know we always share alike."

"If I tell you, big sis, I'll have to kill you," Candace laughed and poured another drink. She gave one to Claire.

"Is this cyanide?" Claire chuckled.

"Always, my big sis," Candace toasted.

"Always Candy," Claire raised her glass. "Well...? Are you gonna tell your big sis how you did that trick?"

"It was a trick I acquired from Melanie, big sis."

Candace found the remote and turned on the exclusive surround sound of the Nakamichi stereo. The built-in wall speakers hummed.

Hey... toot, toot...

Ah... beep, beep...

Toot, toot...

Ah beep, beep...

"Oh turn that up, pump that," Claire screamed, jumping off the sofa and dancing around in sexy underwear. "I haven't heard that in a while."

"Who does this song remind you of?" Candace asked.

The sisters jigged and sang along to the Donna Summer classic.

Bad girls, bad girls talking 'bout bad girls...

Hey mister, do you have a dime...?

Do you wanna spend some time...?

"Who...?" Claire asked.

"This song reminds me so much of Melanie. Remember her?" Candace asked.

"I sure do. Melanie who stopped boosting and now buys all our stuff off Jacque?"

Claire answered. "That Cuban bitch should not be trusted. Remember that."

"Yeah, we're gonna see her in Miami."

"She's working with heavyweights," Claire answered.

"I heard she's big in that town."

"We should pay her a visit."

"Okay, Claire. I'm gonna unpack and send some of this stuff to our fences."

Claire stepped into the large bathroom and joined her sister, squatting naked in the whirlpool.

CHAPTER 6

A couple hours later, the Osorio sisters were on their way to Bungalow. The exclusive nightspot was hopping with paparazzi and club-goers everywhere. A bouncer held the enthused throng of party people behind the velvet rope.

"Pull it up to the front," Claire requested.

A chauffer-driven Bentley stretch eased to a stop. The sisters, dressed to the hilt, stepped out in four inch spike heels. Their tall sexy frames were sheathed in black cocktail dresses. Claire and Candace scowled as people and paparazzi in the crowd wondered aloud.

"Who the fuck are these two...?"

"They must be models."

""Let's shoot them anyway. They may be important stars... "someone said.

"You two are beautiful. Give us a smile...!" another shrieked.

Flashbulbs blared as the beautiful sisters sashayed to the front of the club. The bouncer parted the crowd and greeted them with a smile. Without delay, he waved them on.

The men stationed at the bar stared at the two as they made their way to the bar.

"The usual?" the bartender asked.

Claire nodded. Candace eyes followed a throng of merry makers in the VIP section. They were loudly toasting and having conversations about making big money movie deals. A waiter appeared with a bottle of champagne.

"Ah...did you order that cheap stuff, big sis?"

"You know me better..." Claire shook her head.

"Someone over there sent this," the waiter said.

"Tell the person thanks, but no thanks."

Claire turned to Candace as the waiter walked away. "Cheap-ass white boy," she said, smiling and waving at Huntley Scot.

"He's flushed with money," Candace said. "And his girl is always by his side."

Before the waiter made his way back to the table, Huntley Scott came over.

"Ladies, ladies I'm sorry," he said with a smile.

"Hi," Claire said.

He winked. Candace smiled. "First, I should've made a wiser decision about the drink but the bar ran out." Huntley smiled.

"I hope you give me a chance to make it up."

"What d'ya mean?"

"I've got better stuff back at my place."

Claire and Candace smiled. They knew he was a rich socialite and his parents had millions. The girls loved the thrill of being considered rich. The sisters had also developed problems with drugs and drinks in addition to purloined coats. Even though they were not, just being in the company of people with money gave them feelings of affluence.

"Please join us," Candace said.

They drank the champagne while listening to Huntley chatting about his plans of buying a few restaurants.

"How've you been, Huntley?" Claire asked.

"It's been going so great, I gotta invest some of this money before it goes bad," he joked.

His humor wasn't lost on the girls. They knew of his lineage to his family's long money, but they also knew of his girlfriend, Nicole, who was always with him.

"Are you here looking for investors or..." Candace said.

"No, Nicole's parents try to get in and that whole thing is causing a rift because I don't need anyone else."

"Here's to independence," Claire said.

"You're solo tonight?"

"I'm solo, but she's here watching my every move."

"Why don't you invite her over?"

"You got to be kidding right?"

"Ah, Nicole is cool," Claire said.

Nicole made her way to the table.

"Hi," Nicole said when she reached the table.

"Hey Nicole, I'd like you to meet Candace and Claire."

"We've met before..." Nicole smiled.

"I didn't know you knew them."

A well dressed young blond man came over and hugged Huntley. He kissed Nicole.

"I haven't told you all the A-list ballers I know either. Everyone heard something about these two. Please, I'd like you both to meet a friend of mine, Doug."

"Hi Doug," the sisters smiled.

The bubbly flowed and the party got crunk with the music booming. Everyone in the party seemed to be having fun. When Doug opened his trap, bragging about his great wealth, he never closed it. Claire controlled her annoyance by drinking and not listening intensely. It was hard to disregard this loudmouthed rich boy.

"Being able to satisfy needs is what having money is all about."

Candace and Claire sat all night listening to the rich kids around them gloating about St. Tropez, buying new three million dollar beach front homes and owning restaurants. The ranting of the rich only made the sisters aware they had boosted a lot but gain nothing. They were like poor girls in this group and the feeling grew hard on them, rubbing both in the wrong places.

"When you're able to retire tomorrow and not worry about a damn thing, that's when richness really counts," Doug said, wet from heavy drinking and yapping about his riches.

The night wore on and Nicole grew further away from Doug and closer to Huntley. She was holding her own but Doug completely lost it. The sisters were tired of Doug and his talk of wealth. They were surprised when Doug berated Nicole.

"I knew you just wanted to come to see your man. He doesn't want you, he wants one of these Amazon beauties, but I'm free. Why don't y'all come to my spread?" Doug drawled.

Huntley frowned.

"I second that," Nicole said.

Claire and Candace looked at each other. Nicole wore the smile of a drunk. She was clearly sucking up to Huntley. The sisters nodded to each other.

"Please excuse us," Candace smiled.

"Don't y'all leave me," Nicole said with a drunken drawl.

The men stood and gawked as the women sashayed their behinds away from the table.

"Those sisters are like drugs to an addict," Doug laughed.

"I'd love to shoot sperm in the faces of those two black bitches," Huntley winked.

"Ha, ha... They're nothing but black asses," both men laughed, toasting drinks.

Inside the ladies room, the three women stood in front of the mirror. Nicole looked on as Claire helped Candace with her make-up.

"Is any of them really your man, Nicky?" Claire asked.

"No, I just freak them both," Nicole slurred while adjusting her make-up.

"Oh, they're not from here?" Claire asked.

"No, they're from Connecticut. Doug is very rich and has oil relatives from New Orleans."

"They got money, huh?"

"Honey, they're pedigrees with a whole lot of money."

Nicole could easily tell that the sisters were interested. She lowered her voice.

"Let me tell you, the other day, I went to Doug's place and he had a bank load of money in a safe behind a Japanese painting."

"Sounds like they the ones that we should be with," Claire said.

"It sounds that way to me also." Candace smiled.

"That's what I'm talking about." Nicole joined in.

Outside, the crowd exhaled oohs and aahs as the sisters were whisked away in a black Concierge.

"How was the party?" someone shouted.

"I dug it. It was to my liking," Claire answered with a smile.

They were chauffeured to a spacious and lavish sprawl in Danbury. Inside, they were treated to cocaine and drinks. When all were completely inebriated, Nicole and Huntley were sucking on Candace's breasts while Doug busied himself with Claire. The tawdry sex encounter continued with Nicole's head wedged between Candace's legs while Huntley busied himself with Claire's breasts.

"I'd like to put my dick in your fine ass," Doug said to Huntley while his hands worked their way up Claire's dress.

Huntley was the first one out of his clothes and then Doug followed suit. They both clawed at Claire and moved closer to where Candace and Nicole were making out. Candace's head was thrown back as Nicole's tongue licked the insides of her upper thighs. Moaning was heard when Doug mounted Claire. She reached out, and handed him a condom. He stared at her as if she had the virus. Doug tried to shove his hard dick into her mouth. They sexual saga continued for a few minutes.

Candace shed Nicole and popped up. She grabbed her purse and pulled out her nine. Three naked people were left stunned. Claire quickly undid silk ties and used leather belts to tie-up the victims.

"What're you doing?"

"What?" Huntley asked. "Do you know who I am?"

"A vic right now, baby boy," Claire answered.

"You fucking bitch..." a confused Nicole shouted.

"Shut up, bitch, before I blast you."

"Go ahead, I dare you," Nicole shouted. "I know plenty of gangsters..." Nicole said.

Candace took aim at Nicole and fired, silencing her. Nicole's lifeless body fell in a heap.

"I mean shut your fucking mouth!" Candace said.

"Oh shit, Candace, are you crazy?" Claire shouted.

"I ain't like that bitch anyway," Candace said.

While the girls were distracted, Huntley ran off, trying to escape. Claire fired, hitting him twice as he headed for the door. Blood oozed from his head. Doug jumped and attempted to run.

"No you don't," Candace took aim.

"How'd you want it?" Claire asked him.

The sisters took deadly aim at Doug's melon. He suddenly dropped to his knees and raised his hands.

"Oh please, don't kill me!"

"Where's the money?" Candace asked.

He removed a knot from his wallet and threw it to Candace.

"You're trying our patience. We talking bout the stash behind that Japanese painting." Candace flashed the nine and sweat beads flooded Doug's face.

"I don't know what you're talking 'bout? You stupid bitches better take that money and run. You've already got two murders. I won't press any charges if you take that. There's over a thousand dollars..."

Candace pointed the gun. Doug held his breath. "Tell us the combination or I'm gonna shoot holes in your fucking head, wise-ass." A few seconds passed before Doug opened his eyes. He knew this was beginning of a twisted macabre. Urine flowed freely when he heard the click.

"It's upstairs in the bedroom. I know the combination," he hastily shouted.

"That wasn't so hard, was it?" Candace asked.

"No, it..." he began and eventually nervously released the information they wanted. Then Claire came up with another demand.

"Give it to me backwards, asshole," Claire demanded.

"Go to hell you black bitches!"

A blast to his dome splattered Doug complaints all over the wall. The pair of femme fatale cautiously went upstairs to the bedroom. They took stacks of cash from the safe.

"There's gotta be over half a million here," Claire announced.

"Hmm, good," Candace nodded.

She made a call to Jacque and ate candies as they waited for him. Forty-five minutes later, a black Benz rolled to a stop outside the driveway. A dark skinned man, his eyes covered by shades, stepped out and rang the doorbell. Candace answered the door and Jacque walked inside carrying suitcases of money.

"We got over half million," Candace said.

"And three stiffs," Jacque reminded. "You're all bugging guys. Now y'all gotta lay low until we're able to leave town for awhile. I gotta get someone to come and clean this shitload of a mess y'all made."

"I agree with that," Claire said as they headed out.

CHAPTER 7

Claire and Candace slammed the door of their black Range Rover. They passed a group of thugs pitching drugs in front of the building.

"What's up? This da Bronx, we friendly up here, ma," one hollered.

"Cool, ain't nothing much," Claire answered.

"What's shaking ma?"

"Same ol'," Claire said trying to appear friendly without being weak.

"So what's up with me and you, ma?"

"Negro, please..."

They verbally sparred for a few rounds. The sisters wore wigs and were made up to look different but problems on the streets could bring unnecessary attention.

"You be acting like a dude. Don't let me have to hit you like a dude."

"You talking smack but you know you can't handle me."

"Pull down those pants and I'll show you sump'n."

"Ahight, but if I do you're gonna have to lick my shit," Claire said and all the other fellows along with Candace started laughing.

"She shitted on you man."

"Damn, you ain't had to diss me like that."

Claire and Candace immediately walked away. They had to get away but were awaiting the word from Jacque.

"I wish Jacque would hurry up and get us out of town," Candace said.

"Me, and you both... Living life like this sure stinks," Claire deadpanned.

"We'll call that nigga from a landline," Candace said as they entered the building.

They walked up the stairs and found Jacque and another man upstairs waiting for them.

"I let myself in and saw you from the window. Where'd you go? Lay low means no-show. It doesn't mean going anywhere even if you're wearing wigs..."

"Okay Jacque, save the lecture and just tell us when can we get out of town."

"I currently have the floor. Where did you go?"

"We were bored and went to the movies. We've been cooped up here for a week now."

"That's how things have to go for now..."

"When are we leaving town?" Candace asked.

"Sit, we gotta talk," Jacque said. "Oh by the way you remember Sean? My best friend from school... He's here to help us."

Drinks were served and a couple rounds later, Claire and Sean immediately hit it off. They talked about his time in jail for a jewelry heist he was involved in. The caper had earned him three years in jail. He did a two year bid upstate and had become chiseled physical specimen. Sean was out on parole and enrolled in college while working on construction team.

"You're way better looking now than you did in high school," Claire remarked, feasting her eyes on his muscular physique.

"Enough of this flirting already," Jacque interrupted.

Jacque explained that Sean would drive one transport car to Florida, and the rendezvous points where they would switch cars. Jacque would drive another car. His people would pick up the Range Rover. When all the plans were made, the girls quickly packed overnight bags, ready to go. Jacque wanted to relax and injected music into the set. The drinks flowed. After another hour, Candace slammed her glass.

"C'mon, I'm ready to roll out," she said. "At some point, somebody should stop and get some more drinks."

"I'm with that Candy," Claire chimed.

Claire and Candace headed for the front door. Just before

leaving, Claire turned around.

"Sean, I want you to ride next to me," she requested.

He smiled. They looked deep into each other's eyes.

"I guess you ride with me Candace. Let's roll," Jacque said, opening the passenger door.

"Hooray for chivalry. Two pussy points," Candace laughed. Jacque let his hand brush across her breast.

"Don't be starting nothing, you can't finish," Jacque said coyly.

"Jacque, you know you want this pussy. But we like fam, boy."

"Why you think I'm going for the pussy? It ain't like..."

"Ain't that what all men want from women, Jacque? You're no different. You know you're a sex maniac. You want my chocha," Candace smiled wryly.

"Candace, you gotta stop that thinking like that. It's bad for your nerves, girl."

Jacque pulled off and stopped short behind the small compact Pontiac that Claire and Sean were getting into. Both rental cars were joining traffic.

"Always check before you make your moves, Jacque," Candace warned.

Taking his eyes off the road, Jacque looked at Candace and smiled.

"Oh, you think I can't drive, that's what it is?" he laughed.

"Look out!" Candace screamed.

Jacque quickly hit the breaks, coming close to rear-ending the other car.

"What the hell?" Jacque screamed.

"Huh uh huh... I was saying, look before you leap," Candace said.

Jacque sighed. He saw Claire getting out of her car, and walking back toward him.

"Are you alright, back there?" she asked with a smile. "Take care of my sister. We ain't got time for amateurs."

"I got it," Jacque said.

"I don't know about you two back here."

Claire ran to the lead car and got in. Sean drove off. Through the rear window, their silhouette suggested they were kissing.

"Will she get her tongue from out his throat so he could see where he's going?" Candace yelled.

"You're just mad because, she chose him first. That's what it is, right?" Jacque asked.

"Jacque, even if it is this is family biz. You stay out of it," Candace said to Jacque. She smiled. "What, you think I'm jealous over your silly best friend from high school? If that's what you think..."

Candace felt the Chevy took off with power, snapping her neck back.

"I better put my seatbelt on," she said.

"Yeah, bitch buckle up. Put your seatbelt on, before you catch a whiplash."

"Jacque you're such a..." her voice trailed.

Jacque laughed and steered the car onto the highway. Candace lounged in the passenger seat, enjoying the rush of wind. She eventually dozed off. After about two hours of driving, she awoke.

"We're not there yet?" Candace asked impatiently.

"No, we're still on a Sunday drive, behind them lovebirds," Jacque fumed.

"Jacque, how much do you know about your boy? I mean he's been locked up, and you haven't really seen him in a long time."

"I knew you were gonna ask about that," Jacque said.

"Well...?"

"He did three years. Ah hmm lemme see two years and he just work out and read books. I know that..."

"What is he into, Jacque?"

"C'mon Candace, ease up. Stop being so overly jealous of your sis..."

"Jacque, we've all known each other since we were kids and this guy goes away and comes back out of the blue..."

"Yeah, and...? People go to jail all the time and they come back out too," Jacque said with sarcasm.

"You don't know my sister the way I do. She falls deep, hard and long in a hole of love."

"She's toying with him... Can't you see that?"

"Yeah but I know a different Claire, who becomes attached easy and will get ga-ga over him. And you know what happens when she becomes obsessive."

"All I know is that he was caught selling and did some years. He used to deejay and hustle coke in the clubs. He's in school and working construction and I'm helping him get back on his feet. So what's your fear?"

"I'm looking out for my sister, that's all. I don't want her to be hurt by no jerk."

The ride down south continued. A few hours later Jacque turned into a parking lot of a motel. He parked the car and stretched.

"This place looks like a good place to chill for the night..."

"Not the parking lot, Jacque. Please let's get a room with a Jacuzzi," Candace suggested.

"You'll be lucky if we get cable," Jacque joked.

He came back having secured two rooms, side by side for the night. Candace and Jacque walked arm in arm, heading for their room. Claire and Sean were already inside and Claire was already all over Sean's brawny build. She tore into his flesh like a hungry cat feasting on a kill. Candace could hear the sounds of ecstasy. She raised her eyebrow, walked outside and Jacque smiled when he heard her knocking on her sister's door.

CHAPTER 8

Candace walked into the room and sat down. She watched as Claire kissed Sean deep.

"I want you," Claire said, slipping her tongue into his mouth.

Candace eased back in a chair next to the bed as her sister locked lips with Sean. He looked at her uncomfortably but returned the kiss with passion. He ran his hand over her thighs. She held him back when he tried opening her blouse.

"Be easy," she said biting his lower lips.

Claire laughed and flirtingly touched his cheeks. Sean was submissive. He was under the spell of her seductive power. Claire straddled Sean and helped him out of his shirt. He held her close as she kissed and fondled each of his nipples. She teased him, her tongue licking his lips. He arched his back when Claire sucked on his earlobes.

"I'm kind a ticklish there," he laughed with a hint of embarrassment.

"Hmm, better not let me find out where your weak spot is baby boy," Claire said, kissing his lips. "It'll be our little secret," Claire winked.

Candace saw Claire straddling Sean.

"Did you remember the drinks?" Candace asked.

"Hmm, oh my Candy, I'm sorry. We got some, it's over there, but after you take a look at all this." Claire raked her fingernails over Sean's hard chest.

"He's a big one..." Candace said and left to mix her drink.

By the time she returned, Claire was already sucking Sean's nipples. His body was sprawled across the bed. Claire kissed him all over and she reached down, massaging his crotch.

"You better be careful, he's ready to explode," Candace said.

"Come on."

Claire pulled Sean to his feet. He dutifully followed. Claire held him by the waist, and turned to her sister. "Are you getting some of this?" she asked, spanking Sean on his tightly muscular rear end.

"I guess..." Candace yawned.

"Oh my God, the both of you...?" Sean said with a smile, his erection blooming in anticipation. Candace walked up closer to him. She whispered in his ears.

"Don't get it twisted. I'm only here for the show. So you better perform well and don't act like you scared of the pussy," she smiled, following her sister and Sean into the bed.

Claire pushed Sean on his back on the bed. She pulled his jeans off, turned to Candace and smiled.

"He's packing," she said. Candace licked her lips and sat across from them. She saw Claire reached down gently, stroking Sean's meaty dick. Claire drooled, watching it grow under her gentle persuasion into a long, thick rod.

"Ooh," Sean moaned, relaxing on the bed.

He closed his eyes as Claire massaged his dick. Candace passed her an extra large condom. Claire pulled his drawers off. In seconds, he was naked. His well proportioned six-two frame had even Candace gasping for air. Sean threw his muscular arms around Claire's waist and easily lifted her in the air. She coiled her legs about his six-pack and rubbed his huge thighs. His dick shot up toward the ceiling. Sean looked at Candace gaping at him and her sister sex act and smiled.

"I knew y'all were some sick ass sisters..." His voice trailed when Claire kissed him.

She leapt from his arm and Sean grabbed her, but she easily freed herself. His dick proudly protruded vertically, as if it was sniffing the air. Claire pulled out a condom and slipped it over Sean's purple helmet. She shoved him on his back and mounted him.

"Oh shit!" Sean whimpered.

"I can hear the bitch coming outta him already," Candace groaned.

"Is she gonna join us or what?" Sean asked, glancing curiously at Candace.

She sat on a chair, eyeing them both like she was watching television. There was no clear expression on her face. Was she enjoying the show? He was wondering and kept staring at her until Claire bitch-slapped his cheeks.

Kissing him roughly, she continued riding his hardened dick. Sean was lost in a world of ecstasy. He started moaning and twisting his head side to side.

"Oh yes, oh baby ah, ah, ah yes, you know what you're doing... Yes-s-s...!" he whistled.

Claire slid off and in one motion pulled the condom off. Then rubbing his dick with her hand, Sean pleaded for more. "Oh please, oh my, oh my," he screamed.

Claire slipped his dick into her mouth and sucked. Sean squirmed and screamed.

"Oh, ah, oh, ah, oh..." he squirted all over Claire's soft breast.

Candace's hand was between her legs, manipulating her clit to climax. She took her bra off, held her breast and played with her nipple when she felt the eruption.

"Ah..."

"Had enough?" Sean asked, pushing Claire's head down.

He stroked her exposed ass and, after grabbing and putting on another condom from Claire's stash, entered her from behind. Sean was pumping his dick deep inside Claire. He watched Candace with legs spread wide, fingering her soaked pussy while watching them.

The room was filled with echoes of their passion. Claire and Sean pleasured each other. Candace was lost in her own world, her fingers bringing her own sexual bliss. Jacque slept alone. He awoke early in the morning and left to eat breakfast.

CHAPTER 9

Claire was the first one up. She stumbled out of bed. Sean stirred and watched her. He awoke and chased her around the room and his hardness grew. He caught up with her just before she entered the bathroom. The boy-toy dropped to his knees, attempting to shove his face between Claire's legs.

"Your sex is so good I can't believe it's real. I gotta taste it..."

Claire pushed him back and squeezed her legs together, blocking all access.

"Y'all men are the same? Take, take, take..."

"What's up? You know you make me wanna go downtown."

"I give this up... You don't take it, never! Do we understand each other, Sean?"

He nodded and Claire left him on his knees in front of the closed bathroom door.

Candace was awakened by the nonstop ringing of Claire's cell. She walked over to the leather Prada tote and removed the cellular.

"What...?" Candace answered. "We're not interested."

She closed the flip phone and walked into the bathroom. Claire was in the shower. Candace entered with her. "Some guy called for Jacque to pick up new cars. He asked if we wanted guns too."

"That fool put it on full blast like that over the phone? He's the one who had us up in the Bronx hiding us out then we get on the road and he exposes us. Jacque's slipping," Claire said between applying soap to her sister's body.

"Best believe..." Candace answered.

"That wasn't really smart," Claire said. "He could have the entire police force from North Carolina looking for us."

"That's where we are? North Carolina...?"

"Yep, don't let their smiles fool you. These country folks are just as grimy as New Yorkers."

"You're telling me, big sis? We'll have to check it out," Candace said.

"I don't see any reasons why we shouldn't," Claire said, taking the soap to wash her sister's back. "Let's find out if they're friends or foes. Either way we'll get at these suckers."

"What're you gonna do with what's-his-face?"

"Take him. He a grown ass, he can handle his," Claire smiled.

"He sure can," Candace said. "Enough with the bedroom talk.

Do we even want to include him like that?"

The question soaked in Claire's mind as the shower continued to run. Her sister applied more soap to her back and gave her a deep rub.

CHAPTER 10

The four emerged from the parking lot and got in the car. Sean posted up in the driver's seat. Candace applied lipstick while Claire drove. Sean and Jacque rode in the next car.

"You never told me them two get freaky like that?" Sean said, lighting a cigarette.

"I told you they were different than other bitches you knew, right?" Jacque answered tersely.

"Yeah, you did," Sean smiled, nodding and looking at Jacque. "But that didn't give me any hint on what to expect."

"Different for them means freaky, fucking different."

"I see. Last night was crazy..."

"Say no more. I don't want to hear about it. Just take it as me envying you."

"You mean you still haven't fucked any of them, Jacque?" Sean asked, laughing.

"I used to fuck with Candace but you remember when they set me up with Melanie. That was back in the days with she's still a pretty ass Spanish chick, I still fucks with her. Bang that was it for me, and the sisters," Jacque deadpanned.

The sound of his cellphone ringing immediately jarred him back to reality. It was Claire.

"Are you comfy back there?"

"Yeah..."

"Claire, tell me what you think of this shade?" Candace asked.

"That's hot, sis."

"Y'all two are looking really nice and comfy back there..." Claire said, getting back to Jacque.

"Why we switch up like this?" Jacque asked.

"Your pal, Contessa, told her cronies to call my phone. She's been spreading it that we on the run and need cars and guns. She's got every Tom, Dick, and Harry blowing up my cellphone, trying to sell me guns and cars. What's up with that?"

"I don't know... She did that?"

"She can't be trusted..." Claire said.

"Do you have me on speakerphone?"

"Yes we do. So don't say anything silly. It may cost you."

Jacque could hear Claire and Candace loudly laughing.

"So what we're gonna do?"

"We're gonna pay Contessa a visit..."

"Be careful, I heard she hangs with some shady gringos."

"That's what you heard? Are you sure you haven't been screwing her too?" Candace asked Jacque.

"No, my peeps told me niggas always getting jacked over there."

"You don't say? Only niggas, huh Jacque...?" Candace asked.

"You may not wanna call ahead and say nothing, Jacque," Claire said before hanging up.

Moments later, Claire pulled off the road and drove into a lot. The garage was open but no one was around. Jacque and Sean walked ahead of the girls. They went up a spiral stairs leading them to the second floor landing. The sound of Bachata was loud in the background. Five Spanish men were drinking Tequila while playing cards with a heavy set woman, clad in only bra and panties.

"Contessa, your ta-tas are out..." one of the card-players laughed.

"It is strip poker. And I haven't won a single game yet, Jose," Contessa said, holding her stomach and cackling loudly. She slapped Jose on the head and laughed some more.

"I think you're losing on purpose," another player laughed, and Contessa slapped him also.

"Looks like we have customers," one of the players said, looking up.

"I'm Jose," one of the card players said, walking over to the group.

"We're here to see Contessa," Claire said firmly.

"I'm Contessa," the busty, fake blonde said, glancing up and acknowledging the newcomers. "Mi casa su casa..."

"Our boy, Jacque's a friend of Reggie. And Reggie sent us... We got the money..."

"That's all you had to say," Contessa smiled. "Reggie's name's still alright around here."

The card players huddled together for a few minutes. Claire started pacing back and forth. She stopped, and peeked at the cards in one of the player's hand.

"You've got a dead man's hand," she said interrupting. Suddenly, all the card players looked at her.

"Huh...?" Contessa wondered aloud.

"The pair of aces and the pair of eights you got means you're holding a dead man's hand," Claire smiled.

"Who asked you?" Contessa asked with a cold stare. Silence spread throughout the air.

"Do we have to stand around while you figure what you want to do?" Candace asked.

"No, you could sit your asses down and stop interrupting," one of the men said.

"Hombre, careful how you talk to my sister," Claire warned.

Contessa turned slowly. She threw a shot of Tequila in the back of her throat, gargled and swallowed without wincing.

"You got some mouth on you for a fugitive..." she noted, wiping her mouth with her hand.

"And...?" Claire answered.

"We got your money. We're here to do biz. Let's see the merchandise, please," Candace said.

"And you're impatient, huh?" Contessa said, scoffing at Candace.

"Are we gonna see the merchandise?"

"Y'all some big mouth, boosting-ass-bitches," Contessa retorted.

"What the fuck...?" Claire asked.

"Hey, hey watch your language fat lady. Let's do business," Candace said holding her sister back.

"Jose, agarre las pistolas..."

Claire and Contessa leered at each other when Jose walked away. The stare down continued until Jose returned with a small cache of weapons. Clearing the gambling table, the guns were placed in front of the sisters.

"Damn!" Sean muttered under his breath.

Candace watched Claire picked up a Glock 27, and her lips curled into a half smile. she could tell that her sister liked the sleek black weapon.

"This is my soul-mate..." Claire fawned, rubbing the short muzzle gun.

Candace toyed with the Smith and Wesson 45. Under the

watchful gaze of Contessa and her hombres, she fidgeted with the trigger mechanism of the powerful handgun.

"You have some clean tools here," Candace complimented.

"Where're the bullets?" Claire asked, throwing a wad of bills on the table. Contessa quickly snatched it up, and started counting the money.

"You can have those cases, but it will cost you another few more hundreds," Contessa said, pointing.

One of the men brought a package. Contessa was still busy with the money. She winked and smiled at Jose when she was finished. Claire threw a couple bills down. The busty blonde nodded.

"Sean, please take these tools out of here and you and Jacque wait in the car. We'll be right out," Claire said to Sean, keeping her eyes on Contessa the whole time.

"Okay..." Sean said packing up the weapons and leaving with a brown shopping bag. Candace opened her handbag and removed her lipstick holder.

"Is there a bathroom here?" she asked.

"Si, over there, senora," Jose said.

She walked away and Contessa sat down facing Claire. She removed three bullets from a pouch, and slowly dropped them one at a time. When the third bullet hit the floor, the men made a move. Candace walked out of the bathroom, sawed-off shotgun blazing as the third bullet hit. She blasted three of the card players and Claire hit the other two. Contessa was untouched and stunned, shaking. Jacque watched it going down from a corner.

When he heard the explosion, Sean ran back upstairs, his heartbeat increasing with every step. He busted through the door, fearing the worse. A sigh of relief escaped him when he saw the bodies.

"Let's Go. Don't kill her," he said as Claire aimed the gun at Contessa.

"Please, please don't kill me, don't kill me. They're the ones who were trying to rob you," she pleaded, pointing at the wasted bodies, leaking blood all over the concrete.

"Shut your mouth, heffa!" Candace barked.

"Next time you try to rob anyone, you think twice," Claire said.

"It wasn't me. I swear..."

"Don't try my patience," Candace said, kicking the chair.

The fat blonde promptly fell on her ass. Candace shoved the pump in her face. "Remember this... You owe me," Candace said and walked out.

"It must be your lucky day..." Claire smiled.

They turned and were walking away, when Contessa lifted up one of her tit and pulled out a snub nosed 45. She took aim and was about to pop off.

"Look out!" Sean yelled.

Candace swung the pump around and fired. The bullet scattered the plump, meaty blonde's stomach all over the place. The four ran downstairs and peeled out, hitting the street with speed. At a highway rest area, Claire inspected the new guns while Candace changed positions with Sean.

"He deserved sump'n extra for saving our lives," Claire said with a wink. Candace leaned into the window and let out a shrill laugh. She smirked when Sean got inside the car.

"Y'all are okay?" Sean said, sounding shaken. His voice was barely audible when he shut the door.

"Huh...? I didn't hear ya?" Claire answered.

"Yeah, say it loud, like you did last night, baby boy. Don't tell me you shook up over that little incident back there. It was just us girls against them bad hombres," Claire said.

"I've seen bodies before. But that was..."

"Here now. Don't start acting like you're some type of boy-scout," Candace chuckled, walking away.

CHAPTER 11

"You alright...?" Jacque asked.

Jacque and Sean were inside the hotel, enjoying porn on the television. They watched India and Extacy worked a double team on Mr. Steel. Both their lips were locked around his thick dick. A chorus of moans came from the actors and audience alike.

"Yeah, I'm better, Jacque. But you're right, them chicks are bananas."

"They're like family. I can't talk that way 'bout them. So it's all good."

"What're you talking 'bout, man?" Sean asked.

"Same thing you talking 'bout..."

"I'm just saying them sisters ain't nobody to fuck with," Sean said, gulping beer and going back to sucking Jacque dick.

"Ah, yeah... That's known..." Jacque sipped.

"When they rolled on ah... That fat-ass Contessa and her goons... They bodied everyone up in there. They had that big, fake-ass, gangsta bitch was bawling like a little baby."

"I ain't never seen two bitches—" Sean started to say but Jacque interrupted.

"Whoa, no need for the disrespect," Jacque said, shoving Sean's head down.

"My bad, my bad, but they straight up killers," Sean said, returning to sucking.

"Hmm... Ah yeah... Dumb-ass Contessa was up to her old tricks. When she saw all that cash, she thought she should take it."

"C'mon, you know that foul-ass-Reggie set it up."

"Damn!" Jacque shouted and after busting a nut, Jacque hurriedly detangled Sean's lips from his dick. The knocking grew louder. Sean jumped up and raced to the bathroom.

"Yeah, and now he better be on the run," Jacque smiled, sipping his beer.

The doorbell sounded twice, followed by loud knocking.

"Damn, damn, double damn! I know it couldn't be Candace or Claire. When they go shopping, they shop for days. Who the fuck could be so damn impatient...?" Jacque wondered aloud, limping to the door. "Who is it?"

"It's delivery..."

"Hold on, I'll be right with you," Jacque said with a smile before getting the door. "Don't tell them about this, I've known them for a long time. And I know for sure that Claire would flip if she found out," he said, reaching for a beer. "Want another one?" he asked, handing a can to Sean. They both sipped.

CHAPTER 12

It was warm, bright and sunny, the kind of day that brings shoppers out to the stores. Candace and Claire strolled through a mall on the outskirts of Miami. They removed their sunglasses and walked into the store. Both were dressed in Prada knock-offs. They sauntered through the store selecting Prada items. They carried the clothing to the dressing room. Claire checked for security cameras. She left an imprint of her lips on the glass of the mirror in the dressing room.

"Cool," Claire announced.

Candace pulled out a sensor remover from her bag. They quickly removed the sensors and changed clothes. Candace carefully placed the sensors on the knock off items and exited the room with security personnel watching them closely. They paid for belts and hats to match before leaving.

"Store security was on to us," Claire said.

"I know," Candace said.

"I made a bee-line for the cash register," Claire said.

"Fuck that. Let's go get something for the guys," Claire said.

"Oh yeah, there's Fendi..."

The summer sale was on and the store was very crowded. Claire and Candace found the shirt department.

"I like this, Candy," Claire said, searching for the right sizes.

"Yeah, Jacque is six two and Sean's about six four or so..."

"Whatever the size, I'm getting ready to do this," Claire said, quickly removing the shirt from the rack. "This is mine," she said, attempting to remove the sensor. The security device burst opened spilling ink was all over the shirt.

"Store security is headed this way," Candace informed her sister. Claire was in the midst of removing the sensor from another expensive shirt.

"Fuck that! I'm out of here with these shirts," Claire said.

"Claire we gotta leave right now. The store security people are on their way..."

"Just a few more seconds and I'll be..."

"Fuck that! We don't have time," Candace mused.

"C'mon Candy, I got it," Claire said, ready to leave.

Candace was on her heels and so were the store security personnel.

"Oh shit! They're on to us, big sis."

Candace was hurrying out of the store. They saw the store's security and picked up their paces, heading toward the main area of the mall. Other security personnel joined the store security and closely followed behind Claire and Candace. The sisters started zigzagging through stores, bumping into shoppers. The sisters quickened their pace. Candace spotted a stretch limo with the chauffer sitting idle outside the mall.

"Let's jack that limo," Candace suggested.

The security persons were now running with their communication devices operating at full blast. Claire could hear the squelch of their walkie-talkie as she raced to the parked limousine and hastily jumped in. The driver was in complete shock as two new passengers jumped into the empty backseat.

"We need your car for a few..."

"I'm sorry but I'm afraid that's totally out of the question."

"We have to leave this place now..."

"What the hell?" he exclaimed when Candace pulled out a gun. "What do you think this is? Some kind of a..."

"Jack-move," Candace said and put the gun to his head.

"Ah... I see your point..." the driver said in a trembling voice.

The security persons were very close. Two of them were standing next to the car while four others walked in pairs, searching behind the dumpsters and stairwells.

"Let's go!" Claire ordered.

"If you shut up and drive, I'll let you live," Candace said.

"Is there anywhere in particular you'd like me to take you?"

"Just drive around for a few minutes. I'll tell you when to stop," Claire said.

The limousine rolled out and the security people jumped out of the way.

"Easy, does it," Candace said as the moving car left the security personnel scrambling out of the way. "We don't want to attract unwanted attention."

The chauffer drove warily around for about fifteen minutes with a look of fright all over his face. When the sisters saw that the coast was clear. They instructed him to pull over and walked to the parked rental car. Claire hurriedly drove back to the hotel and both ran into the room with Jacque and Sean still sipping beer.

"What y'all doing up in here?"

"Sipping brew and watching porn of course..." Candace said, looking at the television.

"Just like damn men..." Claire said.

"Let's pack up and get out of here."

"I thought we were leaving when it gets dark?' Jacque asked.

"Change of plans," Claire said.

CHAPTER 13

It was a scorching hot day in Miami. The Osorio sisters had completed another boosting mission. They were in separate cars. Jacque rode with Sean and Candace and Claire were together. They slowed as they passed a mall with Harry Winston jewelers. Claire strained her neck to see the display window.

"Oh it would be heavenly to have items from there," Candace said, peering intensely.

"Yeah, it would be like having multiple orgasms," Claire smiled.

"I wonder if we shouldn't park and..." Candace mused.

"No! After what happened earlier, I think not," Claire finally said.

"Do you think Jacque and Sean...?"

"I don't wanna think about it," Claire said.

"But they look so comfortable back there riding together," Candace said.

"Don't go there, Candy," Claire said.

"That man couldn't be gay, big sis," Candace said with a smile.

"Please get me to the spa," Claire sighed.

"Where are they going now?" Jacque wondered and dialed his cell.

Claire steered the whip into the Hyatt Hotel and retrieved a ticket from the attendant. The sisters entered the hotel lobby area and leisurely walked to the massage room.

"I need a full treatment," Claire said.

"Nothing beats a day at the spa," Candace said as both went inside the reception area.

"You and Sean go get a room and watch another movie," Claire said, answering her phone.

"I could do this everyday," Candace smiled coming out the spa.

"Yes indeed, sis. I don't think I'll ever get another Brazilian wax, ever. But this is bikini land and I gotta look sharp," Claire said, joining her sister.

"I think its sexy shape she designed on you, big sis."

"It might be, Candy. But it's got me itching way too much."

"We better be out then," Candace said.

"Let's see what Jacque and Sean are up to now," Claire said.

"I just know you're ready for some more sex from Mr. Man-of-the-Moment," Candace joked.

"I could certainly go for that," Claire laughed as they stepped on the elevator.

The sisters went upstairs and Claire immediately pursued the satisfaction to her sexual desires.

"Jacque, check the trunk for those guns," Claire said.

Jacque and Sean went out to the parking lot. They retrieved the shopping bag with guns and ammo. Jacque whistled when he saw the girls getting on the elevator. He gave Sean the bag.

"Take this to the room," Jacque said.

He joined the girls in their bikinis, smiling on their way to the elevator.

"Damn, y'all are looking really nice," Jacque laughed.

"What you know?" Claire asked.

"No, it's who do we know. Melanie called earlier," Jacque said.

"Melanie..." Candace said with a smile.

"Funny, we were just talking about that chica," Claire said.

"Her song was playing the other day on the radio, and..." Candace smiled.

"I didn't know. Melanie sings...?" Jacque asked.

"No, but the last time we went to Miami, she always did her routine to *Bad Girls*, by Donna Summers," Claire said.

"Toot, toot... hey... Beep, beep..." Candace chanted and they all laughed.

"Y'all are acting damn crazy," Jacque said.

"I was getting bored and Melanie knows how to get down," Candace said.

"You know how that Spanish heifer gets down," Jacque said.

"Don't hate," Candace said. "Your man, Sean can keep your company."

"I'll call Melanie in a few," Claire said.

"Don't cap anyone, alright?" Jacque joked.

"We'll be by the pool," Claire said. "How's Sean?" Claire asked.

"What y'all did to homey?" Jacque asked with a serious tone.

"What are you talking about?" Claire asked.

"Yeah brother," Candace said.

"Sean is a hard-rock, hard-body nigga. Now he's acting all scared. I don't know what's up."

"He just ain't never dealt with sisters like us," Claire smiled, licking her lips.

"He's a punk-ass, he's not no hard-rock," Candace joined in.

"I mean, he still on parole so y'all gotta slow down with him around," Jacque warned. "He's so nervous he's been drinking up all the liquor since you've been... Are you fucking with his mind too, Claire?"

"Wow! I didn't know I had that effect on men," Claire laughed.

"I ain't his PO," Jacque said. "Anyway, he'll be alright once he gets used to you guys. One more thing, you need to call Mimmy. She's worried about you and Candace."

"We'll call her soon," Claire assured him.

"Tell her we're filming or something. Make up sump'n Jacque. You're good at that," Candace said.

"Yeah, ahight, I'll handle that. When y'all running with Melanie, who's gonna keep an eye on you?" he asked.

"We don't need anyone keeping their eyes on us," Candace said, getting on the elevator.

"Hang out with us for a few and then we'll decide what to do. But you can go back home whenever you want," Claire said.

"What about Sean?"

"Sean...?"

"Yes, that boy-toy of yours..."

"There are two cars, right? Take him back with you," Claire said as the elevator door closed.

"Good luck, girls."

CHAPTER 14

Welcome to Miami

The road sign read. Both Girls relaxed in the stretch limousine as the driver cruised along Miami highway. They had called Melanie but didn't want her to know they had been in Miami all this time and not call. They decided to have her limo driver pick them up at the airport.

"How was the flight?" the chauffer asked.

"What flight?" Candace asked.

"Oh yeah, the flight was great. Thank you," Claire chimed.

"There is a bar on your left. You're welcome to help yourself. Melanie told me to take you to the hotel. You're listed as guests of Uma Mann," the chauffer said.

"Thanks. Hmm, Miami have that fresh money smell," Candace said.

"Yeah, it'll be my chance to relax on the beach," Claire said.

"I hear you, sis."

Candace slipped her large frame Dolce & Gabbana shades back over eyes. Claire sighed as she relaxed in the limo. Melanie had them booked at the Tropicana under aliases. The sisters checked in and quickly got into their two-piece bikini suits and lounged poolside.

"Ah yeah big sis, this is the life," Candace breathed.

"Hmm... Yes Candy, you damn right."

Shapely hips, toned legs, the sisters looked ravishing in bathing suits. They splurged on rounds of drinks and were a little tipsy by the time Melanie showed up. She was dressed in Gucci heels, Cavalli silk hot pants and silk shirt in honey shade. There were lots of diamonds, large ones on her fingers. Smaller ones dripped from the loops on her ears and her lips. Melanie came sashaying over to them.

"Enjoying the lovely sunshine? How're y'all doing?" Melanie greeted.

"Melanie, how're you?" Candace kissed the vanilla complexion, Spanish woman full on her lips.

"Damn Melanie, you're looking really fly. I want you..." Claire joined in, laughing.

"And you're looking as beautiful as ever. Dame mi un beso, my baby." They hugged and kissed lovingly. "C'mon you two, let's talk, and catch up on old times." Candace, Claire and Melanie set off for the elevator.

In the hotel room, all three relaxed on a huge bed. Melanie

couldn't keep her hands off Claire's ass.

"Damn, I need some of this," she said, rubbing Claire's exposed ass cheeks.

"Ooh, I see you're still the wild one," Claire smiled.

Candace poured drinks.

"None for me," Melanie said. "I have to stay sober. I'm seeing a nervous pharmacist in a minute. Later we can really get down."

"What's new with you, Melanie?" Candace asked, giving a drink to Claire.

"The same ol' hustle but different locale," Melanie said.

"You've really grown, Melanie," Claire smiled.

"All the talk back in New York is about y'all asses."

"Really...?" Candace smiled.

"Y'all be soon making the most wanted list for that caper in Connecticut. Why couldn't y'all just suck them rich boys off instead of killing them?"

"That shit just happened. I had the gun in my hand and they were talking shit and I just had to step up or get played."

"Candy just bust a cap in this bitch's dome and shit just hit the fan," Claire added.

"The news said you guys are wanted for questioning in the murder of three Connecticut socialites. Money job..." Melanie's voice trailed.

"You know... We got a little dough..." Claire smiled.

"How much...? Put a bitch down," Melanie screamed.

"Enough to chill out down here for a few and decide where the fuck else we should go," Claire said.

"Oh not to worry, y'all could hide out down here for eternity. Ain't nobody gonna know. I told the limo driver y'all flew in from LA. Ya feel me, my girls? That's how I gets down."

"We hear ya, *Ms. Uma Mann*," Candace mocked, winking.

They laughed easy like old friends do. Melanie was a half- Irish, and all Cuban. She often passed for black, Cuban, Honduran, Columbian, or whatever exotic woman the imagination could muster. After her junior year in high school, she had fled to Miami to live with her father's relatives. They were all in a life of crime and Melanie learned very well from them.

"Anyway Jacque was on the horn telling me that y'all got somewhere close to a mill..."

"Jacque's been talking too much," Candace said as she sipped. "I'll deal with his ass when I see him."

"Oh you two should hook up and stop keeping everyone guessing. How's Mimmy?"

"Ah... As well as she can be, I guess." Claire's voice trailed.

"Mimmy is herself. She's..." Candace started.

"Y'all don't see her much, do ya?" Melanie asked, cutting her off. "Y'all too busy to see her. Admit it. I haven't seen my parents since I started dancing at seventeen. If I had listened I would never have gotten this far. Which reminds me, I have twenty five thousand dollars here for you. There's another twenty five on the way."

"What did we do?"

"This for the jewelry, have you forgotten? It's the Miami air. I got some people who love that shit to give me seventy. I took my cut. And a little went to the limo driver."

"The limo driver treated us fine and all but don't you give up our dough without first consulting with one of us," Claire warned.

"Let's move on, please," Candace suggested.

"Yes, please. Let's move on," Melanie retuned contrite. "What's a couple thousand dollars between friends? I've got a project lined up for y'all. It's so sweet y'all gonna both be licking my ass."

"So much for the job-talk..."

"Oh wow, this is a pleasant surprise," Candace smiled.

"Or should we say, Uma Mann?" Claire teased.

"So there's some money for us, Ms. Mann?"

"That's chump change. I know this judge..." Melanie started.

"You know a judge?" Claire asked with sarcasm.

"Talk about moving up in the world," Candace screamed.

"Wait a minute, I need another drink. Ohmigosh! You know a judge and he ain't sentencing you?" Claire asked.

"Get your drink and when you come back I'll tell you sump'n that's really incredible," Melanie enthused.

"Bring me one too," Candace said.

Claire walked away to fetch the drinks. When she returned, Melanie was gently massaging Candace's round, bare ass. Both were lying on their stomachs with their backs to her. Candace was naked.

"Damn, y'all can't wait for me," Claire said.

They rolled over on their backs and Claire handed a drink to Candace.

"You two are so beautiful. I just wanna fuck y'all," Melanie said while reaching out for Claire.

"What's the deal with this judge?" Claire asked, sitting on the bed. "Have you been stealing his briefs?" Claire and Candace laughed.

"I don't have to steal. He squeals his guts out when I'm spanking him. It goes down every Thursday from eight to ten o' clock."

Melanie and the sisters laughed. "He comes in with his milky, white ass, and by the time he's leaving, that shit is red like tomato. He calls it his therapy," Melanie said and they all laughed.

"You're too much..."

"Are you ready for this? He issued a warrant for the arrest of this dealer, Marco Cortez," Melanie said in a serious tone. The sisters looked at each other.

"Whoop-ti-fucking-doo," Candace said dryly.

"No sis it's more like, 'hoo-fucking-ray' for Marco," Claire shouted.

"Not so loud," Melanie cautioned. "He's in this hotel. The bust is going down later tonight. You two can start kissing my ass when I give you the details on how we make this happen. Two mill in two minutes, that's what I'm talking about. Welcome to Miami y'all."

"Okay and...?" Claire asked.

"Now if they get to him first, well that two million is gone,"

Melanie smiled.

"But if some foxy chicks get to him first, then who to say whose money it is. That two million is ours," Candace said.

"We split it three ways. And more importantly we'll be helping out the law so it's okay for us to keep their cut," Melanie said.

"The judge ain't in on this?" Claire asked.

"Mum's the word in his department. All I have to do is take care of his therapy on Thursdays and he'll be fine," Melanie dryly noted. "Don't be so overjoyed."

Both sisters hugged and kissed Melanie.

"I know there was a good reason for us being here." Candace sipped her drink as she spoke.

Melanie was now massaging Candace's breast. She nibbled at her nipples. Candace arched her back in pleasure. Melanie rubbed Candace's crotch.

"Ah yeah, Melanie, I love this. That's it..." Candace said.

"Don't you think we should be making plans to move in on Marco before the cops get to him?" Claire asked in between sipping.

She sat on the bed watching Melanie licking Candace's breast and saw her sister squirming.

"It's all taken care of. You two are his girls for the evening.

"Now that explains why we're in this hotel," Claire said.

"I have a connect who was able to get me the key to his place. We can pay him a visit. It'll be like back in the days. Remember how we used to rip them drug dealers off?"

"We...? Puh-lease cut the nostalgia," Claire laughed.

"That's the plan... Any questions...?" Melanie asked.

"Yeah, I've got one. What if he doesn't like us?" Claire asked.

"Then he must be gay, cause we're beautiful women," Candace said, shaking her tits.

"If he starts shooting...?" Melanie paused and reached inside her Chloe silver reptile handbag. She pulled out three automatic weapons with silencers attached. "These are all brand new. I brought them just in case. Y'all welcome to choose one," she said and blew a kiss to the sisters.

"Is he around?" Claire asked, inspecting the weapons.

"According to my contact, he's here waiting for an escort service," Melanie said. "He's been calling to the front desk all evening. The guns are in your hands, girlfriends."

"Let's escort the man out of his money," Candace said, hooking her top and choosing a gun. She tucked it in a suede Coach drawstring.

"He's in room 503," Melanie said, carrying a Louis Vuitton monogrammed knapsack.

Claire concealed her gun in a Gucci snakeskin handbag. The bikini clad sisters and Melanie strolled to the elevator. All three ladies were sexy and turning heads strolling through the hotel. The sisters headed directly to the room number and Melanie kept watch outside. Claire rang the doorbell.

They could hear the rummaging inside. Marco Cortez came to

the door, but didn't open it. He waited, before asking, "Who is it?"

"It's me, your escort for the evening. There is no time to waste. Open up. We must hurry," Candace said.

"Hold on. I've been waiting for the past six hours. Don't tell me about hurrying up," he said, opening the door and pointing a gun at the sisters. "How'd you know I'm here? Who are you two? You're not from the same service I used the last time."

"Look, are you Marco Cortez?" Claire said.

"Yeah, I spoke to some Spanish chick. I didn't expect two fine ass black bitches to come here." He put his weapon down and returned to finish packing. "So where are you taking me? I want to go further south where it's so hot..." he started with confidence.

He paused, slipped a cigar out of a case and put it in his mouth. Under the watchful eye of the sisters, the balding man slowly opened a drawer. He reached into it and before he could turn around. The girls had their guns on him.

"Hell would be perfect," Claire and Candace chorused, taking deadly aim.

"Is this some kinda joke...? Ha, ha, ha..." His voice was shaky.

Cortez turned, reaching for his gun but it was too late. The sisters blasted him with two muffled outbursts of their weapons. His body crumpled to the carpet, leaking.

"Let's get this dough," Claire said, already searching the place.

"Under the mattress," Candace said. "Melanie said he was lying on it."

They raised the mattress up and saw two kilos of cocaine and the money.

"Shit...!"

"There's a lot of coke he didn't sell. I wonder who was coming," Candace said.

The sisters opened the door and Melanie walked in with a duffel bag. She paused and examined the place before taking another step. Melanie threw the bag at them.

"Hurry, girls," she said and walked outside.

Melanie was talking on her cellphone when she saw a maid on rounds. She smiled at the busy woman. The maid walked away under an intense gaze of the lookout.

A few minutes later, the sisters came out. Their shades and wigs were in place. They walked quickly past Melanie and entered an elevator. Melanie waited a few minutes then she left. The sisters returned poolside and ordered drinks. They were sipping daiquiris when Melanie joined them. She too was wearing a provocative looking bikini.

"Ooh whew! You look hot," Candace hissed.

"The Cuban fire herself," Claire laughed.

They walked to her waiting limousine and quickly left the area. The trio wound up at a Hyatt not far away. After checking in under various aliases, the trio found the nearest pool and slipped on their shades enjoying the sunshine.

"Welcome to Miami," she said, sinking in a pool chair next to the sisters'. "Now I can have that drink," Melanie announced with a wink and a smile.

Both sisters raised their glasses. There were smiles all around and laughter flooded the air. It had been an easy takedown that netted over a million with cocaine. Claire started to think loudly about the loot and the conversation quickly followed.

"Don't worry about all that yayo. I'll take care of that."

"Let's drink. I'd like to forget about work for just a minute," Candace suggested.

"Here, here," Claire said as more drinks arrived.

"Salu ladies," Melanie said, raising her glass.

The Osorio sisters followed suit. Childhood friends and business partners hugged and kissed like lovers celebrating a reunion. The partying continued into the wee hours of the morning. There was something sinister and infectious about Melanie's ideas.

Early morning on the balcony of the Four Seasons hotel, Melanie held Candace's legs in the air. Her naked ass glistened with sweat as Melanie ate her pussy until Candace wept like a cat. Claire rolled, fingering herself to the tsunami of moans.

CHAPTER 15

Tuesday at ten in the morning, in a busy office in New York City, Sean was sitting outside his parole officers' office for his scheduled appointment. He looked well dressed in an Armani suit and watched the other parolees pitching quarters while they waited. Several parole officers trickled back and forth through the hallway. Finally one of them shouted.

"Gentlemen, c'mon, this is not Rikers. Sean Johnson..."

"Here..."

The parole officer handed him a cup and he followed the PO down the hall to the Men's room. After peeing in the cup, he sat at the desk with PO Martinez, a stocky man with shifty eyes.

"Are you comfortable where you're staying?" Martinez asked.

"Yeah, it's cool for now."

"You got something on your mind?"

"Nah, it's all good."

"Is that a real Armani?"

"Yes, it was a gift from my sister."

"What that cost her... Like...?"

"I don't know. It was a gift, like I said."

"Expensive suit, but nice. Have you been looking for work?"

"Yeah, I'm in with a construction crew, and I got a couple things lined up, while I'm going to school."

"You need to get out there and find yourself a job."

"Yes sir, I'll do my best," Sean smiled.

Martinez studied the record while watching the parolee exit his office. He scratched his head, noting that Sean's caretaker was his sister. He made a mental note that he would pay her a visit.

The next day, the Osorio sisters couldn't resist the lure of satisfying their incurable boosting appetite. They were inside Giorgio's. Shoppers were crawling all over the leather-ware store. The sisters selected items and were preparing to discreetly remove tags from the merchandises.

"Let me handle all the items. I've got receipts and a staple right here," Candace said.

Once all the merchandises were selected, Candace removed the sensors and dropped the items on the floor. Claire picked them up and folded the selected items neatly. She placed the items in a shopping bag. The disarmed security devices she dumped in another shopping bag that was stashed when they walked out the store.

The sisters moved on quickly to Polo. They browsed the shoe department. A salesgirl greeted them. She was all smiles as she went to retrieve the orders. Claire positioned herself on the other side, dislodging magnetic stickers from a pair of riding pants she already tried.

By the time the salesgirl returned, the sisters had already left. In less than half hour, the sisters walked away with more than seventeen thousand dollars of merchandise from Style Lab, Ted Lapidus and Dolce & Gabbana's.

"Let's leave Diamonds for another day," Claire said.

"Sure, big sis. That's sounds like a plan. I see you got some things for boy-toy."

Later that evening, Melanie and the sisters decided to cozy up at a bar on the strip.

"All right ladies, I'll make sure things are set at the strip bar. I'll leave the driver for y'all."

"No, I want to see you strip, sexy mami," Claire said, downing her drink.

"Y'all coming to support ya girl, right?" Melanie laughed.

Candace was shaking her rump on the dance floor with two

athletic looking guys. Claire signaled to her and she walked off. Her dance partners were in a groove and wanted more.

"What's the deal with y'all? I was just getting ready to show the brother how my ass shakes," Candace said, still dancing while approaching the table.

"Melanie has to go to the strip bar," Claire said.

"Aren't you the owner, Melanie?" Candace asked.

"Yeah, but I have to make sure my girls are paid," Melanie said, lighting a cigarette.

"What're we waiting for?" Candace asked.

"I'm rolling with two infamous fugitive sisters."

CHAPTER 16

Meanwhile, Sean was chilling with Jacque in a NYC café, when his cell phone rang.

"Yeah, who dis?"

Sean heard his parole's officer voice and immediately his blood stopped running and he felt like he was about to burst a vessel. He stood frozen, not breathing for a beat. It was the same look he had after being with the Claire and Candace in the shootout at Contessa's. He was shook, like he had just seen a ghost. Jacque eyed him as he slowly walked away, clutching the phone to his ear.

Moments later he returned, nervously fidgeting with his drink and collar. Sean looked like he wanted to say something, but he didn't. After a few sips of his brew, Jacque pushed the issue.

"Everything cool, man...?"

"Jacque, I don't know what da fuck I got myself into," Sean said.

Jacque stared at him, realizing that the level of tension was more intense than he would've suspected.

"Man, whatever it is it's..."

"You don't understand. My PO is trying to drum up some bullshit charges."

"The PO is trying to violate you?"

"My sister said he came around asking questions about where she got dough to buy new Armani suits."

"Why?"

"Last week I wore one of the suits Claire had given me to see him."

"Big mistake, huh...?"

"Yeah, and now he's all over the shit."

"That shouldn't be a problem. Tell him I gave you the suit as a gift. What does he care?"

"I wasn't thinking and told him my sister bought it," Sean said.

The waiter returned with drinks. Sean drank quickly and ordered more.

"Easy, man. You won't be able to walk out," Jacque said.

"Who cares? You can always carry me out."

"You could be overreacting."

"Yeah, but he just called to see me in the morning and reminded me about my curfew."

"What're you gonna do?"

"I'm gonna get drunk tonight and see his fat ass in the morning."

"What're you gonna tell him?"

"I don't even wanna think about it," Sean said, throwing back another.

"I don't see what the big deal is."

"C'mon, you know the system is always trying to come between you and your freedom," Sean said, and drank.

Back in Miami, the Osorio sisters were dazzling in skimpy black dresses, and Melanie was seductively dressed in a red dress. They stepped up in the strip club, known as Mela Bar & Grill. The place was on the outskirts of the city. The owner pranced over to the bar and spoke to the bartender. Then she walked over to where the sisters were seated, quietly sipping martinis.

Melanie dashed from a customer to a waiter chatting them up. The crowd was heavily tourists. Everyone was having fun. A rousing applause was given when Melanie entered the stage to a reggae number.

"I guess she's still got it..." Candace said.

"It's in her blood," Claire said sipping.

"Different strokes..."

Candace raised her glass with her eyes on Melanie's gyrating body. The dancer smiled seductively and did her tribute to the song the girls remembered her by.

Toot, toot ah... Beep, beep...

Toot, toot ah... Beep, beep...

Bad girls...

It wasn't long before the sisters were singing along. The sisters were swept away by their friend's bumping and grinding. They rushed the stage and stuffed dollar bills in the crotch of the dancer's bikini. Melanie took delight, wiggling her ass about the stage.

"Do some pole tricks," Claire demanded, throwing dollar bill after dollar bill on the stage.

Melanie bent over, exposing her crack and mounting the pole. Men and women cheered wildly. The dancer humped and slid up and down on the pole. Her moves tantalized the audience. Melanie went to other customers who were also screaming.

"Melanie, Melanie, Melanie..." the men chanted.

"Oh, she's still the shit..." Candace said.

"Yeah, I'm open and wet," Claire laughed.

After her performance, Melanie kept the same frantic pace, kissing customers and dancing around the place. The crowd enjoyed every minute of it. Finally she made it over to the table where the sisters were seated. The crowd cheered when she kissed them both deeply.

"I can't hear a thing," Melanie said.

"All the screaming and shouting for you drowned all that..."

"You two are a mess. How're the drinks?"

"Hey, slow down, girlfriend," Claire said.

"Yeah, take it down a notch. You're making me dizzy," Candace joined in.

The waiter brought over buckets of ice and champagne. Melanie popped couple bottles, letting the bubbly flow. They drank and partied hard, laughing loudly.

"This spot's really nice and it's hopping too..." Claire said.

"I'm so happy to see y'all. Salu," Melanie said raising her champagne glass. The sisters did likewise. "This looks like a very profitable night. Lots of ballers are here. I'm talking about some Miami Heat ballers, baby.

"Let the deejay shout them out, then we can see where they are," Claire said.

"No, I already told him some people don't like hearing their names, strip club and all. Drink and enjoy ya-selves while I mingle with my fans and make a few extra for the retirement fund," Melanie laughed.

"Go ahead..." the sisters chorused, raising their champagne glasses.

"That damn girl used some of that coke before she got rid of it," Candace observed.

"We owed her that. When you've got judges feeding you info, you're doing alright," Claire said, observing the club. "Seems like some real ballers in here, spending big money."

"I'm tired and my feet are killing me. I gotta go," Claire said.

"Yeah, I'm with you," Candace said.

The sisters exited the club and got in the limo.

"Enjoyed the show ladies?" the chauffer asked in a thick Spanish accent.

"Yeah, it has really been a pleasant evening," Candace said.

"Yes it has..."

The driver was on the way back to hotel, when Claire spotted a bar where oysters were the main attraction.

"Oh, I wanna try that," she shouted.

"Try what?" Candace asked.

"Look over there. They're throwing darts. C'mon Candy, it'll be fun. Let's do it please..."

"Since you're gonna cry, we can try just one game. And that's it. Driver, please pull over there. I'll sample the oysters, thank you," Candace deadpanned.

As soon as the car came to a stop, Claire jumped out the stretch and ran into the bar. Candace hurried behind her. Claire slowed at the door and Candace caught up to her.

"Remember, just one..."

They walked into the crowded bar where a woman was totally embarrassing a loud-mouthed guy. Claire and Candace were watching while she measured his dart and threw hers. The dart hit dead center. She was the winner.

"You lose. Pay up."

"You cheated. You do this for a profession, ripping off good paying customers?" he drawled.

"Pay me. I won fair and square," the girl said.

The man pushed her backward and she fell. She was on her knees.

"Bitch, you ought to pay me for allowing you to play with me," he pushed her face down, slurring.

It was quickly getting out hand and nobody did anything to help her. Claire and Candace looked at each other.

"He's either the mayor or the town's bully," Claire said and walked over with her sister in tow. They went to where the girl was struggling to get up.

"It's punks like you that add to the bad name men have," Candace said, helping the girl to her feet.

"Where're you taking that bitch? You're writing a check that your ass can't cash," he said, stumbling after Candace. "You may be tall but you're too still too weak to fuck with me, you black bitch!"

"You're right, I'm not gonna fight you," Candace said, pushing by him. "My sister will take care of you."

"I ain't scared of no oversized bitch. Where's your sister?"

He lunged at Candace. She didn't look back. There was no need to. Claire caught him flushed with the handle of her gun. She pistol-whipped him bloody. As he lay unconscious, Claire went into his wallet, pulled out some bills and threw them at the girl. The sisters walked away.

"If you can't stand the pain, don't play," Claire said.

CHAPTER 17

The following day the sisters were still in bed when the phone started ringing. Candace answered. It was Melanie.

"Are you up?" she asked. "How's the Four Seasons treating y'all? It must be good because ya sound like ya still laid up."

"Is that Melanie on speakerphone?" Claire asked.

"Yeah it's me. You better be nice before I come over there and whip you both until you call me Melanie Sunshine, like my clientele do."

"What'd you want, Melanie?" Candace asked.

"Rise and shine. It's mid-day, America's most wanted."

"You left me so horny. I gotta get me sump'n long and hard," Claire teased.

"One of those mornings...?" Melanie asked.

"No, we'd rather fuck you baby," Candace said.

"I may have sump'n better for y'all."

"Does it come with a battery?"

"Ya slipping, my girl," Melanie said with a smile. "Ya batteries should be charged and ready."

"Who said we aren't?"

"Ya two are a mess. Why don't y'all clean y'all stank asses and get back at ya girl..."

"I don't know where you getting all that energy, Melanie?"

"That's why they call me Melanie Sunshine. Hmm, hmm excuse me, I have ta go whip some booty."

"Go on girl," the sisters chorused.

Claire and Candace continued to lounge. Claire picked up her cell phone. She dialed Sean. The call rang through to his voicemail.

"I'm not leaving a message. I'm not his," she said.

"He might be banging the next one," Candace said, walking to the bathroom. Claire got up and followed her into the shower.

"Give me a back rub," Claire said. "I need my bones cracked."

Showers pelted the streets of Manhattan. It had been a dry summer but today, it rained all morning. Sean pulled his Sean John black summer jacket closer and walked swiftly into the parole office. He fidgeted with his new Gucci wallet, compliment of Claire, tapping his heels, he waited in high anticipation. His parole officer walked passed him. The officer paused, looked down on him and shook his head.

"Follow me," he ordered red-eyed, carrying a cup of java.

Sean stood lazily, yawned and did as he was told. He continued down the hall that led to a small interview room. The PO ushered Sean inside and invited him to sit. He held the coffee cup to his lips and sat on the desk. Sean stood watched him put the cup to his lips while looking over papers on his desk.

"Sit," the PO ordered before sipping. Sean obediently followed and squatted.

"You've got one chance to level with me, Johnson," he started and Sean knew where he was going.

"Look, I lied about the suit. It wasn't given to me by my sister. A friend gave it to me."

"Are you lying now? I could violate you now but we'll see what happens," he said, picking up his phone and dialing. "What's the name of your friend?"

"Jacque..."

CHAPTER 18

"Hey, we're supposed to be on a vacation," Claire protested.

She was outside the storage place that Melanie had rented for them. The sisters notified Jacque, and he coordinated the delivery of the sisters' bounty to Melanie. She had a team of Mexicans stocked the place with stolen items, everything from clothing, cases of liquor, and electronic equipment. Melanie walked in and stood next to two new Harley-Davidson motorcycles in the middle of the floor.

"Now this is what I'm talking about. Why isn't there three of these babies?"

Melanie waved her arms around the huge storage. "Look at all this. Oh my God! I mean check out those king-sized California oak beds and those huge arena size screens. I just have to get sump'n on my commission. Tell me whose credit cards bought all this."

"Mr. and Mrs. I-won't-tell..." Candace chuckled.

"You can have some of the leather gears," Claire said, sitting on a beautiful marble stand. "That's enough of a commission for your work."

"Yeah, you don't really look like you lacking, so don't take too much. The motorcycles are for us," Candace said, squatting on a thick beveled-edge, glass table.

"So, are y'all ready for sump'n else?" Melanie asked moving closer to the sisters.

"You didn't hear me mention us being on vacation?" Claire asked, staring coldly at Melanie.

"Let's listen to the judge's therapist," Candace smiled, examining a bottle of Louis XIV.

"We got another job?" Claire asked, looking at Candace.

"We don't have to do shit, we don't want. Shoot, we could just do what those old mobsters do."

"What's that?" Claire asked.

"Retire right here in sunny Florida."

"Enough of the damn sibling rivalry already... It's this easy. Ya either gonna do the job or ya not. That's all there is to it," Melanie said, sighing. "You two, what I got to be Mimmy too?"

"I haven't mentioned it yet, but you're close to an ass whipping," Claire threatened.

"I'm ready," Melanie said, grabbing her tits and licking her lips.

"Let's do this for fun. It better be easier than the last one. I don't want anyone killed," Candace said.

"The last one was cake-walk for y'all," Melanie said.

"All righty then... Break it down."

"A certain movie producer with long and loaded green pockets would like a certain actress..."

"Okay, it sounds difficult, already," Claire said, throwing her hands up.

"Well, Jacque told me y'all were trying to get into acting and I feel this might be ya big break."

"I swear, Jacque talks too fucking much," Candace said.

"Like I was saying, I figured this movie producer will meet his actresses..."

"He's gonna meet us but don't blame us if he don't like our skills," Claire said.

"We're really not that good..." Candace said, sounding embarrassed.

"Y'all very beautiful, and ya both can still carry a damn conversation, can't ya?" Melanie asked. The sisters shook their heads. "Fuck it, ya still in. Here's how it's going down... We just need to be around this fat cat and get real close to him. Let him show interest, then bam. We take the cheese and run. Now I'm a tell you how we do this..."

The Osorio sisters drew close and listened to Melanie outlining the plan to rip-off the movie producer. He was also connected to the mob and loved beautiful, dark skinned women. The sisters listened and thought the plan had a chance. They didn't come to Miami to work, but job after job had found them. Claire thoughts drifted to Sean. She felt eager to see him.

"This man has no brain. Matter of fact he lets his dick leads him around," Melanie said.

"I'm surprised that Sean didn't pick up his cell earlier," Claire wondered aloud.

"It's a man's prerogative."

"I can't believe ya two are discussing dicks in the middle of my plan to make us some dough?" Melanie asked. "Y'all are ridiculous. This is preposterous. I'm hungry."

"Yeah, let's go and find someplace to eat," Candace suggested.

"I know an absolutely exquisite place."

"Did you learn those words from the judge?" Claire teased.

They laughed and headed out the storage area. Two young Cubans followed Melanie and the sisters out. They locked the storage area and walked away.

"What's behind the warehouses?" Candace asked.

"Oh that's the Keys, baby. All along here is the entrance to the Caribbean and a whole new world, baby."

"Yeah Miss Sunshine, let's go," Claire said.

The girls were in a good mood as they got into the limo and were off to discuss their plans over a big lunch. A few minutes later, the limo pulled to a stop outside Sardi's and the girls walked in.

After their meals, the girls cruised the strip in the limo. Candace and Melanie were kissing each other passionately while Claire sat with her hands rubbing between her legs.

"Damn Candy, you and Melanie are making my ass so hot and horny," Claire muttered, rubbing her loins.

"Spoil-sport... Do you want me to get the chauffer back here?" Melanie asked.

"I need someone with a large pussy-soother," Claire laughed.

"Okay, okay big sis, why don't you call that buffed-ass dude? What's-his-name?"

"Yeah, I think I will call Sean," Claire said, pulling out her cellphone and dialing.

"Yeah fly him here, immediately," Melanie said dryly.

"Keep jumping each other, and I think I will fly him down."

In New York, Sean was working out in a downtown gym. Sweat poured from his hard body. His cellphone rang. Sean quickly set the weights down, wipe sweat off his brow and answered the call.

"Damn girl you're gonna live a long time. I was just thinking about your fine ass. For real, girl...!" Sean enthused. "I wanna see you too, but money's kinda funny. Cool, I'll get permission from my PO and I'll be there. Hmm, what tonight...? I seriously doubt that. I'll let them know it's a family emergency... Don't worry baby, I'll get there... See you later, mu-ah," Sean said, making a kissing sound with his lips.

Around nine in the evening, Sean exited a flight out of LaGuardia, New York City to Miami International. Claire and the chauffer were there to greet him at the airport.

"How was the flight?" Claire asked hugging him.

"I love flying baby and first class was really off the hook," Sean said, kissing her passionately.

"Anything for you," she said.

Claire pulled him back to the limo. Sean threw his overnight bag in the stretch and sat next to Claire. They embraced. His hands were roaming all over her body.

"Damn girl! You living," Sean said, glancing around. He saw the bar and smiled.

"All Melanie's idea... You'll meet her later."

"Seems like you've stepped it up a notch since you been out here, huh?"

"Yeah, this is plenty different than NYC," Claire said, checking the Gucci on her wrist.

He grabbed her and squeezed her tight in his arms. Sean kissed her neck and both cheeks.

"I hate quickies..." she smiled, wetting her lips with a snaking motion of her tongue. "Let's talk about you..."

"What's that you said about a quickie?" he asked.

Before Claire could answer, Sean was kissing her moistened

lips, and the nape of her long neck down to her back. His lips roughly brushed against the hollow of her throat. She reached between his legs and teased his package. Sean was rock hard and rearing to go. Claire wore a devilish smile.

"We're invited to a launching party tonight," she said, and sucked his lower lip into her mouth.

He couldn't stand it anymore. He had to have her. Sean pulled her skirt off and sat her in his lap. Claire reached down and held his hardened dick.

"Huh uh, not so fast, sweetheart. I may want you as badly as you do me, but I'm running this, okay? Plus we've got time on our hands."

Sean fell back while Claire went to work undoing his shirt. She sucked on each nipple while her fingers gently stroked his dick. She watched as he winced from almost exploding in her hand.

"Uh ah... Please let me have some," Sean begged, writhing in pleasure.

He licked his lips and tried not to disturb her movements against him. She easily slipped a jimmy-hat on him. Then he felt the incredible friction while they made out, she had mounted him. It felt like heaven. Sean moved in time with her rhythm, thrusting as she rode. Booties collided and Claire manipulated his love muscle until he held her ass, ripping her apart.

"Ah... Oh my... Yeah...! Baby, baby, baby...!"

It was as if a dam had exploded. He held on tight, kissing Claire's lips while riding in the sunshine. Then he watched as she rode uninhibited, her desires hemmed, followed only by passionate groans. She raked her nails across his chest.

"Uh, uh, yes-s-s, oh yes, baby... Oh yes-s-s...!"

Claire's head jerked back and she opened her mouth as if to scream, but no sound escape. Her nails continued to rake his back.

"Ooh shit..." she moaned, kissing him slow.

Claire sat in his lap hugging him close. Her body shuddered with lingering tremors of delight. She kept sucking, biting on his lips long and deep.

CHAPTER 19

Later on a huge yacht, a promotional party was being thrown by Dominique Bonelli and his partner Maurice Tines, co-owners of Son-Tines Entertainment. Melanie introduced the sisters and Sean to the many celebrities in the Miami area. The Gala was serenaded by a band. Soon after, Dominique Bonelli walked on stage and greeted everyone in a flamboyant manner. The sisters raised their eyebrows and nodded.

"Ladies and Gentlemen, I'd like to thank everyone for coming out to this shing-dig sponsored by Son-Tines Entertainment. Feel free to eat and enjoy yourselves at the bar. Remember people, tomorrow the year's number one movie will be released by Son –Tines Entertainment, me and my partner Mo Tines." He raised a diamond encrusted mug and yelled. "Tomorrow brings a new day for Son-Tines Entertainment."

Whistling and applause erupted in the full house. Then an older man joined Dominique on stage. They greeted each other with a kiss that appeared clumsy. Again, the sisters raised their brows. They started watching Dominique's behavior closely and became slowly convinced there was more to Dominique and Mo Tines' relationship than met the eye.

"It's great to see the support and this is the kinda support we're looking forward to see when the movie is released. Thank you all, mazol tov!"

A deejay had the soiree jumping. Guests were hopping and clapping to the latest mixes. Champagne flowed and the party-goers were living it up. The sisters spent time schmoozing and getting closer to the top movie gurus. They were finding out what was behind Dominique and Mo Tines' relation. Looking closer, they saw not only the shaved eyebrow of both but also similar huge yellow diamonds in their pinky rings.

"This is a money meets money type of affair. Damn, it's crazy in here. When did you meet these big ballers?" Sean inquired.

"A friend of a friend..." Claire said. "C'mon, you're talking too much. Let's make-out on the dance floor."

When they returned, they saw the large framed, Dominique Bonelli. He was drinking and chitchatting with Melanie. Candace winked at Claire and smiled.

"You must be the other sister I'm supposed to meet, beautiful. Are you enjoying yourselves?" Dom said, greeting the newcomers.

"Guilty as charged. This is a friend, Sean," Claire said with a naughty smile. Dom extended his arm and Sean shook his hand.

"Nice to meet you, Sean," he said and turned to the sisters. "You're both as beautiful and sexy as Melanie described. And if you're even half the talent she claimed, I'm certainly looking forward to working with both of you."

"We would love to work with you also," Candace said.

"Thanks for the confidence," Claire joined in.

"Give me a chance to introduce you to my money guy."

"Are you for real?" Claire asked.

"I'm real, honey," Dom answered.

"Okay, let's," Candace said.

"I'm afraid I can't do it right at the moment."

"Ah...and why not...?" Claire asked sounding disappointed. "This might be your only chance to show how *real* you are and..."

"My partner was ah... Seasick and had..."

"Well, there it is, our chance," Candace said with a chuckle.

"Give me some room here. He's throwing a little party at his estate tomorrow. It's real exclusive and if you give me your address I'll be more than happy to send a limo your way."

"We got our own limo," Candace said.

"Your own limo...?"

"Yes, we've got it like that," Claire laughed.

"What do you know?"

"Who do you think we are...?" Claire started.

"Yo man, they'll be there," Sean said, interceding.

The sisters and Melanie stared at Sean in wide-eyed surprise.

"Okay, Mr. Bonelli, me and my sisters will be there," Candace said and turned to Claire with a glare. "Will excuse us please? We got some ah, urgent matters to take care of."

"Sure, I'll see you tomorrow evening," Dominique Bonelli smiled and moved on. Melanie locked arms and walked away with him.

The sisters pulled Sean out of the earshot of other partygoers and laid down their objections.

"Listen, don't you ever speak unless you're spoken to. In case you forget, you're here for the dick work only. Now keep your fucking trap shut!"

"He didn't mean anything by it. Be easy with him, Candy..."

"Here, clean up after your baby," Candace said. She angrily walked away.

"Candy is mad disrespectful... She had no fucking right..."

"First of all, I'm the only one who calls her Candy. And secondly, you fucked up, Sean. Don t you ever talk out of turn again, ever," Claire said.

Her lips were on his mouth and that silenced any further protesting from Sean. They walked to the upper deck and watched the stars.

"It's still a beautiful night," he whispered in her ear. She sat on his lap and could feel his bulge at work.

"Let's take this back to our room," Candace said, walking over to them. "We're about to dock."

The three walked down the steps of the yacht and into the waiting limo. Sean sat next to Claire with Candace facing them. He was all over Claire, kissing her hands and her shoulders, biting her neck. She fought him off and giggled as he forced himself.

"Hmm... Easy, big boy," she groaned when he sucked her earlobe.

He was panting like a dog in heat for her by the time they hit the hotel lobby. Pawing her and groping her all over. Claire didn't fight. She allowed him to take her easily in his wild passion.

"My feet hurt," Claire whined.

Candace handed her a look of disgust as Sean scooped Claire off her feet. He easily carried her on his muscular shoulder through the lobby and to the elevator. They were deeply kissing by the time they were inside the room. This time she let him take charge. He poured kisses all over as she lay in the bed. Then he carefully took her clothes off. When she was naked, he buried his face between her upper thighs.

"Oh Sean," she screamed and squirmed in delight. She raised her long legs and rested them on his shoulders. Claire sighed and guided his sheathed head into the crest of her moistness.

"Yeah, take this dick."

Sean thrust himself inside her. His balls slapped angrily against her raised ass. He tossed her back and forth, spanking her ass when he threw her in the doggie position. Her butt cheeks glistened with sweat. He licked her ass and sent his tongue curling up her asshole. Claire shook her head when he rammed his dick back and forth inside her.

"Oh, baby yess! You're fucking me just right! Hmm yeah, keep this up and I'm a have to keep you closer... Ah, ah..."

Candace, sitting a few feet away from the action, watched while fingering herself. She smiled when she heard her sister's tumultuous explosion.

"Oh yeah, oh, yeah, oh Sean..." Claire grabbed his head and moaned.

"Ah!" Sean groaned.

It turned him on when he saw Candace watching and massaging her exposed nipples. He watched before plunging his dick deep into her sister's gushing pussy. He was still thrusting deeper and deeper. Candace threw her head back and spread her legs.

"Ah..." Her fingers expertly fondled her clitoris.

Claire clung to his powerful thighs, pulling him deeper inside her. Liquid pleasure oozed down her legs and groans spilled from her lips.

"Sean, oh yes!"

CHAPTER 20

They sisters awoke the next afternoon. Sean wasn't around. Candace wandered through the hotel room and lounged in a chair on the balcony.

"Have you see Sean?" Claire asked.

"No, did you give him permission to go outside?"

"No, I didn't. He must've been bored. We did sleep the whole day away."

"Let's go down to the pool," Candace suggested.

Both girls put their bikinis and sunglasses on. They walked down to the pool and immediately spotted Sean on his cellphone. Claire waved at him. He quickly put away his cell phone and returned the wave.

"It seems like men are always running their mouths," Candace noted dryly.

"He's probably bored," Claire said to her sister as they approached Sean.

"He could be calling the next woman."

"She couldn't treat him the way I do."

"It's about the conquest. You should know."

"Let's see. Hey there Sean, who've you been calling, baby?"

The sisters sat down on either side of him. He laughed nervously and looked at other revelers at poolside. Claire and Candace stared at each other with their brows arched.

"See, my sister has a thing about trusting men."

"I have a lack of trust for some men and you fall into..."

"She thinks you've been holding out and keeping another woman—which is all right if you are. I told her she was wrong. You secretly crept out of the bed and that leaves her talking..."

"I don't have another girl."

"Hoo-fucking-ray for me," Claire shouted, pumping her fist.

"So who were you on the phone with?" Candace asked in a serious tone.

"I was embarrassed to say it at first, but it was just my lil' homey. I was telling him how beautiful it is and all... I think... I mean I love the place, so far..."

"Say no more, Sean baby. My sister is a sore loser. Last one in the pool is a chicken nugget!" Claire yelled.

Sean went running then dove into the water. Claire followed behind and Candace put her headphones on. She watched them for a minute, closed her eyes and chilled beneath the pressing mid-day sun. Claire and Sean frolicked in the pool for a couple of minutes. They soon returned to the comforts of the poolside chair and cocktails.

"It's almost time to meet with Dom's partner," Candace said when they sat down.

"It is. Enough of this playing around."

Claire giggled as Sean held her and tickled her sides. "Wow. I had a great day too, Sean. Tell your friend about that the next time you call," Claire laughed. "So we're gonna meet the money man, huh sis?"

"Yeah, let's go look our finest," Candace said, getting up and fetching her things.

"What about me?"

"What about you?" Candace turned and asked.

"I mean I'm here and I thought..."

"Your job is to get..."

"Yeah I know. Tighten up your sister and 'we'll take care of you,'" Sean mocked. They left him at the poolside. Candace was sure he would make another call.

That evening, as promised, the sisters were whisked away in a waiting limo courtesy of Dominique Bonelli. They were radiantly dressed in black silk Armani dresses and four inch Prada heels. Their necks were draped in pearl. Both were ravishing when they stepped out of the limo and sauntered through the doors held open by an obliging doorman.

"Good evening ladies. The activities are on the main floor to your left," he announced, bowing several times.

"Thank you," the sisters chorused.

"This is real money," Candace said.

"You don't say," Claire said.

The place was decorated with white orchids. A long table sat beneath a huge crystal chandelier. The guests were well dressed in evening suits and dresses.

"I'm glad we came well dressed for this occasion," Claire said, looking around the room.

"Happy to see that you two could make it," Dom greeted the sisters as they sauntered into the hall. All eyes were on them.

"Good evening, Dom," they both chorused.

"This is great," Dom said as he took their arms and led them to a bar filled with drinks. He poured three glasses of champagne and handed one to each sister.

"Long live wealth," he toasted and sipped.

"Here, here," the girls chorused and did likewise.

"Your partner must be a real nice guy," Candace said.

"The best," Dom said. "He's building a huge bungalow on the beach. When it's finished, all the parties will take place there," Dom said, laughing and sipping.

"Will we be invited?" the sisters asked, smiling.

"At the very top of the list," Dom smiled.

They walked to the table where three men were seated, drinking and smoking cigars.

"I want you fellas to meet two beautiful, talented young ladies who are destined to be our next stars. Gentlemen, meet Claire and Candace Osorio," Dom said, waving his arms.

The three men stood and applauded like fans. The girls smiled gracefully and bowed. When the men saw how fine they were, their applause grew louder.

"Thank you very much," Candace said.

"I'm Mike Deberi," one of the men said, kissing both girls. He was adorned in diamonds around his neck and wrists. A very colorful man, there was a lethal charm around him. His gold tooth was revealed when he unleashed a broad smile.

"Huh!" Candace said when she felt his hand all over her ass.

"Sensitive..." he smiled.

"Why do they call you Goldie?" Claire asked, quickly coming to the aid of her sister.

"I always wear them..."

"I see," Claire said, looking down and smiling.

The other two men looked on disinterested. They were distracted by a man with slick black hair, sporting a pink Channel suit and matching Hermes shoes. He was loudly talking and snapping on everyone. He appeared tipsy.

Claire and Candace sat next to Goldie and his men. The loud mouth and his entourage walked by the table.

"Who is he?" Claire asked when she saw Dom running behind the man.

"Are you talking about the big shot over there?"

"Yeah..." Claire smiled as she spoke.

The mood was light. The mobsters laughed and looked the sisters over again.

"Was it something I said?"

"I thought you recognized the host with the most, Mo Tines. That Jew has money and he's financing that entertainment ring that your pal runs. He tends to be a drunken playboy. I'm sure he's already sizing you two up."

The sisters watched Maurice Tines chatting up other men in dark suits. His uncontrolled gait spoke of his state. In an underworld of crime and power it seemed odd to the sisters that he was given a lot of respect. With Dom and two cronies hanging on, he finally staggered over to the sisters and sat down.

Goldie and his crew stood. Before walking away, Goldie stopped and briefly spoke with Maurice Tines. Maurice Tines seemed to listen intently. He then brushed Goldie off.

"So you two are the Osorio sisters," he drawled. A crony lit the fat Cuban cigar dangling from his lips. "I want you girls on my team. You're both indeed beautiful," he said and kissed each sister's hand. He chuckled.

"Enlighten me here, please. Who is who?" he asked puffing. He waved his hand and another drink appeared.

"That's Claire and ah..." Dominique Bonelli started to break them down.

"Dom, let me talk to the ladies, okay? Why don't you go get a drink and leave this type of work to me, huh?" He waved, dismissing his business partner. Dom dutifully walked away and left the sisters with Maurice Tines.

"Oh, don't worry about us. We can handle ourselves." Claire smiled.

"I'm Candace and she's my sister, Claire," Candace said, moving closer.

Maurice Tines talked freely about himself and his wealth. He started in the racketeering business fifteen years ago as an enforcer. He was a blue-collar man, who had risen up with a perfect accountant's mind. Maurice Tines ran his organization with brains. Dominique was clearly the muscle. Mo Tines, as he was affectionately called, controlled six posh nightclubs all over Miami and Vegas. He wanted to be the center of attention. Then Maurice Tines bragged about feeling hate coming from one side of his own camp.

"Now all I carry are my trusted friends," he said. Maurice Tines pulled the suede bag out and produced two golf-ball sized, blue diamonds. They sparkled when he rubbed them.

"Why do you carry those stones...?" Claire asked.

"They have to be extremely expensive," Candace surmised.

"These diamonds, I'd rather keep real closer than any amount of cash. Why?" he asked, and then proceeded to answer his own question. "Because money is dirty," he chuckled.

"We never quite looked at it like that," Claire said.

"People are always chatting up their money," Candace said.

"Yeah, people shit on money, vomit on it. It's dirty all the way round," he said. The sisters feigned interest in his philosophy. "Cash belongs in banks. Diamonds are a guy's best friend." He glanced at the object of his desire and his eyes settled on the sisters.

"That's certainly good to know," Candace said.

"Listen, you two's are fucking beautiful. Why don't you both come to my clubs sometime?" he said. Then pulling the sisters closer to him, he continued. "I'll take good care of you and if you like, then hey, you can take care of ol' Mo," he laughed and the sisters shared his joke.

"We'll take you up on that offer real soon," Claire whispered in his ear.

"I've been told that I have a legendary hard-on," he laughed.

"That makes it an invitation we can hardly turn down," Candace said, playing along.

"We wouldn't miss it for the world, Mr. Maurice Tines," Claire said.

"Okay then ladies, it's a done deal."

Maurice Tines departed with the assistance of two of his flunkies. He made his way across the room. Back at the bar, he held court. Goldie and a flunky watched him carefully. Claire and Candace sipped on drinks and listened as Goldie schemed.

"He's ripe for the picking," Goldie said. "Are the boys in place?"

"Yes boss. We'll hit that drunk as soon as he leaves the place."

"Good," Goldie said.

Two hit men walked outside and sat in the cool Miami air and waited. Dom left first and jumped into a car driven by one of his associates. Then Maurice Tines and four of his men walked out.

They helped Mo Tines in his car and the other two men walked to another car. The shooting started when they got in the cars. Automatic weapons lit up the early morning skies. The two men shooting at the car occupied by Mo Tines cleared the streets.

The car with Tines swerved and careened out of control, crashing wildly into a hydrant. It was deadly still for a minute. Then the hydrant exploded. Water sprayed all around. The driver was hit. A flunky jumped into the driver's seat, backed the car out and floored the accelerator. Tires screeched and the drunken mob boss's car spun out, disappearing down the road.

Coming out of the club, Claire and Candace heard the commotion. They quickly ran to the waiting limo.

"What happened?" Candace asked the chauffer, jumping inside.

"I don't know. I see Mr. Tines walking with his boys and then boom, fireworks like it was the Fourth of July."

"Mr. Tines...?" Claire asked with curiosity. "Are you sure?"

"Si senoras... I'm very sure. He's a popular man in Miami."

"Really...?" Candace asked.

"He's Ms. Melanie's boyfriend."

"You don't say?" Candace mused.

"Well, we certainly learned a lot tonight," Claire said.

"Hmm, hmm, you can say that again."

CHAPTER 21

The following evening, the sisters along with Sean, were carried by limousine to a posh nightclub on the strip. They were ushered in by beefy security guards and walked into a flamboyantly decorated place. The dress code was upscale and celebrities poured in. Candace walked in front while Sean and Claire made their way in. The place was jumping. A female rapper rocked the microphone. Sean and Claire joined the revelers who were setting it off on the crowded dance floor. The crowd was grooving and partygoers did their thing.

After the rapper ended her show, house music pumped through the loud sound system. Candace was already dancing with Mo Tines when Claire and Sean caught up to her.

"Hi, Mo," Claire greeted the man wearing a green Armani linen suit. "You're looking handsome."

Maurice Tines spun her around and took her in his arms. He kissed her deep. Sean was clearly taken back by this, and clenched his fist to prevent himself from lunging at Tines.

"This is my friend, Sean," Claire said, recovering from the passionate kiss.

Sean hesitated but finally opened his fist and reluctantly accepted the handshake.

"What's up?" he said, pumping Tines' arm.

Drinks flowed abundantly and the sisters, Sean and Maurice Tines spent the night getting wet. During this time, the sisters found out that both Mo and Dominique were always together.

Claire and Candace found out that they weren't only kissing buddies but both were sexually involved with each other. The sisters were into the sweet-talking Mo Tines and were listening intently to his boasts.

"I'm kinda tired. Why don't we go back to the hotel and have our own private party?" Sean whispered in Claire's ear, trying to steal some of her attention.

The sisters were lavishing all their interest on Mo and his conquests. They were ignoring Sean, who was eager to receive some attention. He nibbled at Claire's earlobe.

"Claire honey, lets get outta here and—"

"I'm not ready yet, Sean. If you want, you can be a good boy go back to the hotel and—"

"I'm not leaving without you," he snarled.

"Temper, temper..."

"You think I'm some cheesy ass nigga, don't you?"

"Why Sean... I never..."

Claire seductively danced away. Two other guys suddenly joined in the fun. Sean danced embarrassingly by himself for a few beats. He watched with mouth wide open as both men got up and under Claire. She wore a smile of satisfaction. Sean watched for a minute and thought Claire was enjoying herself too much without him. One dancer clung to her long shapely legs while the other worked her ass. They were double teaming her.

Sean watched with a half smile when Claire opened her eyes and glanced his way. His smile quickly turned to a frown when she looked away. Sean felt his anger boiling after two more songs. He felt played by the two dancers. Sean danced over and pushed the dancers away. The music was blasting when they tried to punch Sean. He caught the dancer in motion and Sean's fist crashed against the dancer's ribs, knocking him down. The security rushed to the sight of the melee, breaking it up.

"You're coming with me..." Sean was loud, out of control and grabbed Claire's arm. She threw her drink in his face. Sean wiped his face and stood. "You bitches think you run the world, don't you?"

"Hey, hey, take it easy. What kind of ugly manners are you displaying around beautiful people?" Tines asked.

"Muthafucka..."

"Be very careful of what you do. You moolies from NYC are

nothing but garbage dressed in pretty rags."

"You talk that shit and you're liable to get your face smashed!"

Maurice Tines' henchmen moved in when he stood. Claire stepped in to break up the fracas but Candace held her back. There were three henchmen. They jumped on Sean as soon as he flexed. The henchmen had him on the floor stomping him. Then they dragged him out the club and tossed him to the pavement. The partying continued without missing a beat.

"You gonna get yours, and that goes double for you Claire and Candace! Y'all two dirty-ass bitches will see!" Sean screamed.

He was in pain and blood trickled from his mouth. Claire and Candace gathered themselves after the scuffle. Maurice Tines held them both and apologized.

"I'm truly sorry about that. Sometimes we don't know how our friends are gonna act," he said.

"We can't agree with you more," Candace said.

He signaled and the busboy raced over, cleaning up in a flash. Next the waiter brought a bottle of champagne.

"Let's have a drink to your beauty," he said, pouring the bubbly.

Out on the strip Sean walked and chatted on his cellphone. Then he went to the hotel, picked up his bag and left. Before getting on the plane, he called Jacque from the airport.

"This is Sean... Man your girls just fucked me over. Right now, they're hanging with mobsters. Home-slice stood around watching about six o' them muthafuckas throw me out the club... I'm fitt'n to hop on the plane back to NY... You gonna call them right now, and call me back? A'ight, I'll wait for your call..."

11:45 pm LaGuardia Airport, the flight from Miami landed and Sean quickly hopped off. Walking quickly through the terminal, he caught a cab and headed for Jacque's. He was definitely in an angry mood and couldn't wait to see Jacque after immediately arriving in New York City. He raced upstairs to the apartment and Jacque let him in. He was swallowing shots of Vodka while talking about the episode that happened in Miami. He was getting drunk, his fears surfaced and Sean started talking loosely.

"They're trying to pin those bodies all on me," Sean said, beating on his chest. "Me, Jacque, me... There were at least five bodies back in North Carolina with that fat bitch and her peoples, man. If I go to jail, I won't be coming back. Shit's crazy!"

"There weren't that many bodies. You're gonna get through this. Ain't no one seen you shoot no one, so what's the worry?"

"My PO is itching to violate me. I'm headed back where I never wanted to go. Shit's fucked up from fucking with 'em bitches!" Sean shouted, slammed his glass down, and walked out.

Jacque pulled out his cellphone and dialed a friend. He wasn't anticipating this type of reaction from Sean, but he was prepared to handle it.

"That nigga is too emotional," he said aloud. Then he spoke on the cellphone. "Teresa baby, my man is coming through tomorrow. Check him out very carefully for me. All right, good looking..."

Jacque hung up and went back to chilling. He was sipping Vodka while watching porn.

CHAPTER 22

The following day the girls got really friendly with Maurice Tines. He invited them to come and spend time on his yacht. The girls spent the day drinking and soaking up the sun on a large boat.

"Riches come in different ways," Claire said.

"Riches without brains is nothing," Maurice Tines said.

"I want to take back this feeling of being there," Candace smiled and stretched.

Later that evening, the sisters were guests of Maurice Tines. He was holding court. The beautiful Osorio sisters were on each of his arms and he was going all out to impress them. All three were putting the finishing touches on another bottle of expensive champagne. Claire on one side and Candace on the next, he filled the ladies' glasses. He hugged them and kissed their cheeks often. He giggled like a schoolboy whenever the sisters slapped his hands.

Claire's cell phone rang. She looked at the call and recognized Jacque's number.

"Got to take this..." she said, walking away. "What's up...?"

Candace stared in anticipation as Claire continued on the phone. Her expression went from a smile to frown. Candace knew it wasn't good news.

"Yes, Candace's here... You wanna speak to her? Okay..."

Claire handed the phone to Candace.

"What's popping?" she asked and listened. After a couple of minutes on the phone, her expression also turned sour. "Don't worry, we'll handle it," she said. Candace glanced at Claire and continued listening. "She'll get over that..." Candace clicked the phone closed. She stared at her sister in silence, until Maurice Tines opened his mouth.

"Is there something wrong?"

The sisters remained silent.

"We're friends. Your problems are mine."

"Claire, we better leave now," Candace said. Her tone sounded grave.

"Right now...?"

"Yes, I'm afraid so," Candace said standing. "I'm afraid our pet back home is sick," Candace continued with a wry smile.

Maurice Tines and Claire stood. She started to gather her things.

"Let me know something. What kind a pet problem you got? I

can always recommend a good vet."

Candace was already walking away, ignoring him. Maurice Tines wasn't convinced. He pressed Claire.

"Take this piece of info... I understand women's independence and all that rah—rah, but certain things are best handled by the man. Such things like, for example, getting rid of garbage, you get my drift...?"

They walked to the door and Claire turned and kissed him on his cheeks.

"Nice show..." she whispered.

"Anytime, and come again."

"We will again, soon." Candace waved. The bouncers opened the door and the sisters strutted out.

"What's with the dames, boss? They got sick or..." one of the henchmen asked.

"I don't know, just my luck. Damn pets...!"

"What kinda pet they got, a dog I bet?"

"I don't fucking know and I don't care." Maurice Tines watched the strut of the Osorio sisters. "But I do know classy asses when I see some, and they got it."

There was a soft wind whipping against their motion. Hair-blowing in the wind, Candace signaled for the driver. When the stretch pulled around, the sisters jumped in.

"Leaving early?"

"It was cool. Please take us home," Candace said curtly.

The chauffer raced along on the highway, heading back to the hotel. Candace stared at her sister.

"Sean's a rat."

The word dropped like a bomb. Claire's expression twisted from surprise, then anger, back to surprise. Nothing was said for a long stretch of time.

"You're saying..." Claire started.

"Your boy-toy has been squealing on us to his parole officer. Jacque said a parole officer came to him and casually mentioned us. Jacque dug a bit deeper and his informant told him they're getting ready to set up some kind of team and Sean's a part of it."

The information rolled off her tongue like poisonous venom shot from a deadly snake. Claire felt the betrayal crawled through her veins, cutting off her breath. She leaned back then sat upright, repulsion dogging her thoughts. She wanted to shut it out but couldn't. She thought of their lovemaking and felt him all over her, dirtying her body.

"A rat...?" she repeated gravely. "No, not my Sean..."

Claire was clearly hurt by this new revelation. Images of the two of them hugging, kissing and fucking ran repeatedly in her mind. She shook her head, but the memories stayed the same.

"If you would only listen to me and keep your fucking legs close, we wouldn't be in this mess," Candace said, looking at her sister's face.

The pain she saw made her want to take it all back, but it was too late. A frustrated and angry Claire smacked her sister's face hard.

"I may be a lot of things but I'm not a whore. Don't you ever talk to me like that ever again," Claire said angrily.

"I'm sorry..."

"Not as sorry as that sucker-ass nigga's gonna be," Claire said with determination.

Claire was furious. She pulled her gun and rubbed the barrel. She checked the magazine and slapped it back inside. She screwed the silencer to the muzzle and looked over at Candace.

"I'm sorry, Candy. I lost my nerves. But thinking how that scumbag played us because of me... Well I sorta lost it momentarily. I'm back." The sisters hugged.

"We're gonna be alright, big sis," Candace said in her sister's embrace.

"Where's that sucka now?" Claire asked.

"He visited Jacque after he left the airport. Jacque told him to chill out. But, big sis, he's back in NY."

"Candy, call Jacque and have him wait for my call. Tell him how worried we... I got. And I was broken up about him leaving... Blasé, blasé... I want him to come back here and I'll take care of him."

"Jacque said Sean was really pissed. He was whining about how we did nothing when he was being kicked out of the club," Candace said as she dialed Jacque.

"Fuck that piece a shit! He was getting on my last damn nerves. Lucky for him I didn't know then what I now know. I would've had him taken out with a bullet. The nerve of that rat," Claire hissed.

CHAPTER 23

It was sunny today in New York City. Sean packed his bag. He felt that he wouldn't be coming back. He waved at his sisters and walked out to the morning air. Sean rode the subway downtown and walked to the parole office. He was set in his mind that he would be ready if they sent him back up north. Sean was prepared to do whatever it would take not to go back. He was taken aback when his PO seemed pleasant when he greeted him.

"Come on inside the office."

The real surprise came when he walked into the office. It was teeming with detectives and federal agents. His heart sank as he looked around the room. The PO was grinning like he'd just won a bet. Maybe this was his promotion party.

"Take a seat," he said to Sean.

Sean dropped the bag and several officers rushed over and immediately scooped it up. They opened it and examined the content. The long interrogation process began the moment he sat down.

There was an annoying quiet. It disturbed him. Sean bent over, putting his face into his hands. What could he say that would make this right? He couldn't bring back lives.

"I don't know nothing about nothing..." His voice was emotional, and he slurred like a drunk. He wasn't convincing. "I don't know anything..."

"Contessa Mendez's people fingered you. Why did you kill her? Is it because she's a woman, Sean? Remember that incident, Sean?"

"Yeah, yeah, I remember. But I really wasn't involved."

"Then it's time for you to save yourself and help me out. I'm sure you know that I'll put in a good word for you. I guarantee that you won't be touched," the detective said.

Sean grabbed his sweaty forehead as if he had a massive migraine headache. He stared at the detective. His mind was playing tricks. He wanted to make it different.

"All right, I mean, I wasn't actually there. I was waiting in the car."

"Were you the driver on this one?"

"It wasn't like that..."

"Okay Sean, let's see where loyalty lies."

The photo sketch, with the title boosters along with pictures of the Osorio sisters was placed in front of him.

"Do you know these two?" she asked.

Sean stared at the picture. He glanced at the sketch. Then he went back to the photo.

"No, I mean they looked very pretty and all but I don't know all the pretty girls in NY. I mean..." he said, sweating as he lied.

The detective pulled the snapshot of Sean and the girls and puddles of water drained from Sean's body. His shirt became wet and perspiration covered the chair he sat on.

"Who are these women to you, Sean?" the detective asked, shoving the photo in his face. Sean stared at it and quietly cursed the day he met the Osorio sisters.

"The one to the right is my girl, Claire, and the other is her sister." His answer was sheepish.

"I can't fucking believe this, you knew these two all along and..." the PO started, but the detective waved his hand silencing him.

"I didn't know what was happening... I..."

"Lover boy, these two are wanted on various charges. Associating with known felons..." The PO stared at him.

"I swear I didn't know..."

"Your girlfriend and her sister are involved in murder. They are notoriously known around town. It seems you've been getting your rocks off with cold-bloodied murderers."

"I didn't know anything about that," Sean said.

"Sean, lying may cost you your freedom."

"They picked me up from the club. I didn't know them like

that."

"They've been riding around town lifting everything that's not tied down and now they've moved on to murder."

"Don't let me find out that you're lying."

"I'm not..."

"When and where will you see your girlfriend again?"

"I don't know. She usually calls."

"Oh, you're just a boy-toy?"

"I ain't nobody's boy-toy!"

"That's on you. Just know the next time she calls you, you call me." The detectives stood. "Play along or we'll put your ass away for a long time," he warned.

By time he got out of the parole office, it was cloudy and the rain came. Sean walked out of the station. He felt an uneasy queasiness in the pit of his stomach.

Sean stopped to get a bottled-water and checked his messages. He breathed a sigh of relief, and hurried to the bus stop. Sean left and Teresa was on her cell phone dialing Jacque. She was a good informant to Jacque and ran down Sean's activities while at the probation office.

"He was in here for about an hour talking with the detectives alone... They had your girls' file and all..."

Jacque closed his phone and thought about the news.

"That muthafucka was snitching on my girls," Jacque sighed.

CHAPTER 24

3pm EST Miami

Claire and Candace were inside their principal warehouse on the outskirts of the city. The place was filled with stolen merchandise. They picked up new weapons and loaded clips in magazines. Candace closed her cell phone.

"Jacque said a detective came by his place asking for Sean."

Claire continued loading the magazine and checking her weapons.

"I'm taking these four babies right here," she said.

"What we should do is bring him back to Miami and take care of him here," Candace said.

"Done deal..."

"Let's go take down loud-mouth," Candace said.

"Uh huh, we'll catch him at his lil' honey's pad..."

"They won't be ready for this."

"Hell no, they won't..."

Red Gucci and Prada backpacks were in place. The sisters strapped the saddle bags to the frame and mounted the motorcycles. They cranked the engine. Claire twisted her long hair into a bun and slipped the red helmet on. It matched the color of her motorcycle.

"Osorio sisters, forever," she said, cranking her engine.

"Ride like the wind," Candace smiled.

She donned the yellow helmet, the same color as her motorcycle. They geared up and set off down the road with speed. The next morning the sisters were sitting idly at a light. They spotted a Starbucks and decided to get coffee. Claire and Candace parked the motorcycles close by and walked into the Starbucks. They ordered their cups of coffee and sat behind another patron.

"This kinda good," Claire sipped and smiled.

"I have this strange feeling like sump'n ain't right," Candace said with a frown.

"What're you talking about?" Claire scoffed.

"I feel a little uptight, like oxygen isn't circulating right..."

"You didn't pay your bill..." Claire joked and sipped. "This vanilla coconut is just right. You should've gotten it instead of..."

"I'm serious, sis. I just don't feel right," Candace said with finality.

"Well you know you're very superstitious so don't let that get you carried away. I called Mimmy and let her know we were doing a modeling gig in Vegas and would stop in Miami..."

"It has nothing to with Mimmy and what she thinks, sis."

"Then what's the matter, Candy...?"

"I really don't know. I don't, but it doesn't feel right, big sis."

"I tell you what, we'll go and say bye to Melanie and clear with what we got now, okay Candace?"

"Lately I've been having all these dreams about dead fishes and..."

"Here we go with all this dreaming again. Candy, I'm sold. We'll pack up and leave for Sin City as soon as possible. Just don't bother with the dreams. They make me nervous when you talk about them."

"Okay..."

Sheryl Street woke up with the anxiety stuck in her throat. She couldn't wait to get it off her chest. It had been building since the day her mother left home and never returned. Now she was working as a police officer while studying law at a local university. She had acquired all the tools and skills required to track her mother's whereabouts. Sheryl was up early, her heart beating rapidly through her chest. She pushed the coffee cup away and walked to the bathroom, her mind weighed down by her emotions. Sheryl hurried through showering and quickly dressed.

In complete police uniform down to her shiny boots, Sheryl walked uneasily to the address of the South Florida mental institution in Chattahoochee. The research she had done and the late evening work had finally paid off. The bittersweet success of her investigations revealed that her mother was mentally ill and for the past sixteen years had been receiving treatment for an acute case of catatonic-like delusions.

Her mother's condition was too confusing for the local clinic when she was living with her in Opa Locka. The day she disappeared, a visiting physician covering for the clinic's doctor who normally gave her medication, recommended confinement for the patient's own safety. For her own reasons, her mother had failed to list Sheryl as a daughter. Sheryl's mother had been confined in the mental institution since she was seven. Now a matured woman, Sheryl entered the building. She was exhausted from not sleeping. Trying hard to pull herself together, she addressed the physician who greeted her.

"Sheryl Street, right? I'm Dr. Katz."

"Yes, I'm Sheryl," she answered, accepting the older woman's handshake. "Thanks for your help in helping me find my mother..."

"Oh, it was my pleasure to help," Dr. Katz said. "This way please..." she added, leading the way through secured doors.

Sheryl caught up with her. Dr. Katz turned her head, eyeing Sheryl. With a smile she said, "Oh so, you really are an officer, huh?"

"Yes, I am," Sheryl feigned a smile.

She could sense the fear around her. The place seemed to belong in some other world. Sheryl had dreamed of the day she would see her mother. There was much to discuss and talk about. There was anger, rage and discontent stirring inside of her, but Sheryl was overcome with sympathy when Dr. Katz spoke.

"She may not recognize you, so be very patient. Her mind is that of a five year old at times when she does come out of her silence. Please try to understand we're doing all we can, but mental illness is complicated. And, if not caught early at times, can become more complicated. There are no proven treatments for her disorder," Dr. Katz said, pointing to a woman sitting alone on a bench and walking away.

Sheryl was stuck in awe of the person before her. She looked much older, gray haired and wrinkled, but there was no mistaking her. The grown woman playing with a child's Barbie doll was her mother. Sheryl was dumbfounded and didn't move for what seemed like an eternity. Finally after discerning the entire situation, she walked over to the bench.

There was fear written all over the patient's face. The scent of urine alerted Sheryl's senses. Her eyes roamed for help when she realized her mother had urinated. Nurses on hand came to her rescue, taking her mother away. Sheryl flopped on the bench in shock. Sheryl left with no further interaction with her biological mother.

Her thoughts were heavier as she drove back to the precinct office in Dade County. Still dazed from the visit with her mother, Sheryl walked into the office and flopped down at her desk.

"The captain wants you in his office," a voice said, interrupting her recollection of the morning's earlier meeting.

Lt. Cooksey was already there in the captain's office, sitting and smiling. She stared at the captain and wondered if she was being brought up on charges for insulting Lt. Cooksey again. He always had a way of pushing her buttons and in the past she had cursed him and had once slapped him. Their relationship wasn't healthy but the job funded her dream to complete law school. Although she enjoyed working for the police, her real feelings were that graduation couldn't come fast enough.

"Sir, you wanted to see me?" Street asked.

"Yes, c'mon in Officer Street... C'mon in and sit down. Now, I know you know Lt. Cooksey, right? He's currently heading up a special task force. Apparently New York cannot handle their trash so this situation has been dumped in our lap. And we intend to show everyone that we can handle it. We aim to clean it up and we think you can help. We need you on this one..." the captain said with a frown of business all over his grill.

When he was finished outlining exactly what had to be done, Sheryl Street was in more shock than when she had walked in.

"You can handle this mission, now, can you Street? Cause if you can't, we'll get those girls and all their connections," Lt. Cooksey smirked.

Street sensed the sarcasm that question came with. She was

confident she could do the job. For a beat, she wandered if she was suffering from the delusions her mother had. She comforted herself in a sarcastic smile when she replied.

"Yes sir, I can. Will that be all?" Street asked and got up.

"Remember, Street. These individuals are well connected and are considered armed and dangerous. Be careful. And don't make any moves without informing either myself or Lt. Cooksey, okay?

"Okay sir," Street agreed with a salute.

"Go get 'em!" the captain said. "There's promotion in this one, officer."

Sheryl left the office, went back to her desk and got on the horn to New York. She started dialing Mimmy's number. It rang before she heard the outgoing message. She left a message for Mimmy to call her back. She next dialed Jacque's number. She was sure he knew and tapped the desk as she waited for him to answer her call.

"What's good...?"

"Why didn't you lemme know that Claire and Candace was in so much damn trouble," Street almost shouted. She quickly resumed her official capacity and continued with less emotion. "I found out all about it from my captain just a few minutes ago. Jacque tell me what you know and help me to help them before any further harm is done."

At first Jacque was unsure, but eventually complied after several minutes of Sheryl explaining to him that she wouldn't tell anyone and would keep everything he told her confidential. He revealed the location in Florida where Melanie had the girls living but didn't give the exact address. He did give her Candace's telephone number. Sheryl immediately made the call from her personal cellphone. The outgoing message came through loud and clear. Sheryl left a message for her stepsisters and hung up. She continued the conversation with Jacque.

Later that day, Mimmy called and after pleasantries were exchanged, Sheryl told her that her daughters were in a heap of trouble. Mimmy wanted details but Sheryl promised to call back. She didn't want to be the one that gave Mimmy all the bad news about her daughters. Jacque was right. Mimmy had no idea about what was going down.

It was late in the evening when Claire called. At first she didn't know who it was, but a few words later and she knew it was Sheryl.

"Please, you and Candace have to meet with me as soon as soon as possible," Sheryl suggested.

Claire agreed and set the meeting later in a restaurant in a busy part of the city.

At ten in the evening, they met at the Capital Grille restaurant. Street was nervous and she opted to wear civilian clothes, a skirt and blouse with heels. Both girls walked into the busy restaurant and all eyes were on them. Claire and Candace looked really relaxed like they were on vacation, but Sheryl knew they were on the run. The sisters were up to no good.

"How did you get my number, Orphan Annie?" Claire teased.

"Well first of all, I'm no longer an orphan or whatever you might think."

"Testy, testy now...?"

"I found my mother. That was the reason I joined up with the police here. It was to find my mother."

"Well good for you," Claire said.

"That's great, but you still didn't say who gave you big sis' digits," Candace said.

The trio was completely unaware that they were being watched by another diner who was secretly taking snapshots of them and straining to eavesdrop on their conversation. She applied lipstick and listened while examining the photos of Candace and Claire. The undercover detective covered the photo with a newspaper and looked at the file when the waiter took her order. She called in for backup when Candace whisked by on her way to the bathroom.

Armed and extremely dangerous, do not approach without backup.

The results were text back in a jiffy with precaution. Candace sashayed by and joined the others sitting at their table, about two feet away from the detective. Her palms were getting sweaty and her fingers itched. She wanted to arrest the sisters, but knew that Sheryl Street was an officer. The undercover detective got the update from the central command. The detective received the news via cellphone. It was confirmed that Street and the sisters had lived under the same roof.

Street was unaware of this silent observer. Out of some unexplained loyalty, she felt compelled to do everything she could to help Claire and Candace Osorio. Yet she chided herself for thinking this way. They were on different sides. The sisters were known fugitives, and she was an officer of the law. There was a dire need motivating her to help them. The sisters however, were protective of each other and refused her help.

Several ideas flooded her mind as she watched the girls sipping wine. All the time Street was trying not to be obvious with her concerns. She was so focused on the sisters that she didn't see the patron sitting behind them, tilting the mirror at an angle to get a better view of the trio. The undercover officer made her move toward their table.

"Did Orphan Annie...? I'm sorry... Did Sheryl say how she got your number, big sis?"

"Yeah Candy, she said that our boy, Jacque, gave her the number," Claire deadpanned.

"I can smell a cop..." Candace said and arched her eyebrow, signaling to Claire.

"If that's the case then you know what time it is..."

Claire and Candace inconspicuously reached for their guns. Giggling and clowning, they seemed to relish the heightened tension of the moment. For Street, time froze as the eatery transformed into a potential shooting gallery. Guns were drawn and other patrons became nervous. But for the Osorios, it was as if nothing was wrong.

"Hmm, hmm..."

"Oh yeah," Candace nodded.

The sisters turned, displaying their artillery. The move caught Street clutching her service piece too late inside her handbag. Candace turned and Street caught her by the arm and sent her flying with a kick to her midsection. Candace landed like a rag doll on the floor. She bounced up with blood in her eyes. The other diners and staff ducked as the fracas erupted. Claire held her gun on the undercover detective.

"I'll blow you away, cop," she hissed.

During the scuffle with Candace, Street's pocketbook fell and her gun was still inside. She tried going for it, but it was too late. Candace had recovered and was on her.

"Bitch, don't you know you can get smoked..." Candace said, rushing forward gun in hand.

Claire grabbed Candace by the arm. The restaurant's staff and patrons began racing to the exit. The sisters stood back to back with guns trained on the undercover detective and Street. She had no gun.

"Claire and Candace Osorio you're under arrest for... Murder..." the undercover detective yelled.

"You will die cop bitch before I go anywhere!" Claire shouted at the undercover detective.

Neither was backing down, but when Street pulled out her badge out, and marched into the scene. She stood between the undercover detective and the sisters. Both Claire and Candace's guns were now pointing at the undercover detective. The detective finally lowered her weapon when she realized that she was outgunned.

"Stay out of it! Or else you will eat lead too, cop!" Claire shouted at Street.

"Give it up. Please don't do this Claire..."

"Shuddafuckup Orphan Annie...!" Candace yelled, lunging forward with her gun. Claire held her sister off.

"Turn yourselves in. This may be the last chance for the both of you. They know all about, the murders you're tied to... I can make it simple for you two, even make a deal. Don't throw away your lives, for what? You're still who you are in the end."

"Well, if ain't Orphan Annie, always trying to help us. You brought the law here?" Claire asked.

"I told you, big sis, not to meet with her 'cause she would set us up."

Street came too close and Claire let her have it. A right fist smashed her grill. Street collapsed like she had been hit by a Mack truck. Candace hit the undercover with the butt of her weapon. The sisters quickly picked up their handbags and walked calmly to their motorcycles. Street recovered quickly and picked up her pocketbook. She ran outside with her gun drawn, but put it away as the girls rode by. The meeting had gone awry.

"I told you I smelled a cop," Candace said when they were stopped by a red light.

"Forget her. Let's go make some money with a mob stoolie, then we're leaving this country..."

When the light changed, they revved the motorcycles' engines and zipped away. Dipping with the sun drenched streets of Miami. The girls rode with the wind in their hair. Like predatory animals, Claire and Candace smelled blood. The sun had completely set and they were intent on making a killing before leaving.

The detective, whose cover was now blown, radioed in for backup to hurry. She reported what mode of transportation the sisters had, then she raced off.

CHAPTER 25

It was a quiet Miami neighborhood. Affluence lurked at every turn. Orange color streetlights lit the way as the two motorcyclist pulled over by the pristine Tudor styled palatial confines. A black Concierge and a F1 McClaren blocked the driveway.

"Is this the end of the road for us?" Candace asked as she removed her helmet.

"This gonna be the last job for a minute," Claire said, removing hers.

"Yeah, I heard what she was saying. We're really notorious like Melanie has been saying, huh?"

"Speaking of Melanie, we're gonna have to mail her cut to her."

"That bitch is one crazy-ass..."

"Yeah, but I think we're crazier, sis," Candace said.

Unseen by the sisters, a parked car was off on the other side. The passengers were in the cut, keeping an eye on the sisters. Claire and Candace walked to the front door and checked their guns before ringing the doorbell. A henchman raced over, listened and knocked on the bedroom door.

"Can't you tell that I'm busy?" Maurice Tines screamed. He was engaged in a screaming match with his girlfriend. The man waited as the argument raged on.

"Ya say ya from the old country, but ya only know modern ways. Ya always running around with these dumb ass whores. I don't want no parts of ya. When is ya divorce gonna be final?"

"Melanie, no matter what, it's you I love, my sweetheart. I only beg you forgive me... I'll never ever do that again." He was contrite but it could've been the liquor.

"Ya swear?" Melanie asked.

"I put this on my mother's head. God rest her soul." He made the sign of the cross and kissed his hand.

"And please put away those blue diamonds," Melanie said.

Maurice Tines pulled out the suede bag containing the huge diamonds.

"You mean these?" he laughed. His henchman returned.

"Boss, some broads outside insist on seeing you," he said.

"Get rid of them, get rid of them now."

"But boss..."

"What's the matter?" Melanie asked. "Your girls come to my home to see you? You dare to bring women to my home?"

"I'm telling you it must be business that couldn't wait..."

"What're you waiting for? Let the women in."

The henchmen ushered the sisters into the home. Melanie stood holding Maurice Tines by his arm. Her negligee was silky, revealing her voluptuous tits and round ass. The henchmen lead the sisters to the bedroom door.

"Stay there. Don't you dare come into my bedroom... This is what you've resorted to Mo, fucking the moolies?"

"It's not like that. Why are you here?" Maurice Tines asked the sisters.

"We're here for the diamonds," Candace said.

"My security here will put your dead bodies out..."

Melanie jumped, scared out of her wits, and her negligee fell to floor. She stood naked next to Maurice Tines. The henchmen were distracted by her nudity. Maurice Tines turned to cover Melanie and Candace blasted both henchmen. Too preoccupied, they dropped, spitting up lead.

"Like I was saying, the diamonds..."

"Don't kill me," Maurice Tines begged. "I'll give you the diamonds." He pulled the suede bag and threw it at Claire. "Take it and leave me alone. But remember. You just signed your own death warrant. My people will hunt you down forever... I... Oh... Ah..."

"Oh did we?" Claire asked and blasted.

Maurice Tines' body was left twitching on the plush carpet. She bent down and removed his expensive watch and bracelets.

"Ah-he-e-eh...!" Melanie shrieked. "Let's get out of here," she said.

"We rode the motorcycles."

"You rode motorcycles? I don't believe this, the two richest bitches in south Florida and they riding motorcycles. Listen up, why don't you come by the club later and..."

"Too much heat in Miami," Claire said, raising her hand.

"We have some business to settle with a fucking rat right here in Miami."

"Ya don't fucking say...?" Melanie asked. "Alright, then do what ya gonna do. Tie me up and take advantage of me. Here take the keys to my BM. The police are sure to be looking for y'all on motorcycles..."

Melanie was hardly finished speaking when Claire clocked her. She fell out, writhing in pain. Then she slumped as if asleep.

"I hope you didn't kill her," Candace said.

"I don't think so. Melanie is tough."

The sisters ran outside and saw the silver BMW. They raced toward it and hit the remote. Not far away, there were men sitting in the car and watching the sisters jumped in the car.

"Goldie, I think them girls saved us the embarrassment of killing that dick face."

"It certainly looks that way. You may just be right."

"What're we gonna do now?"

"Why don't you call him and see what happens. Ha, ha, ha..."

The mob crony dialed his cell phone as the sisters peeled out.

"Goldie, those moolies are getting away. What about the plan?"

"Fuhgeddaboutit! That two-timing bitch hasn't answered the phone?"

"No boss. Maybe them bitches had balls and killed her."

"I don't think so. She said she was running this. She told them what to do..."

"Hey boss, here comes the cops."

"What's the matter with them? They went straight to the motorcycles."

"Hey Goldie, you think we should help the police out and tell them the girls aren't in the house."

"No, fuhgeddaboutit. Let the police do have fun doing their job. That's what they're paid to do. Then we'll have a meeting and take over dick-face's turf. Fucking faggot deserved to die anyway. We'll settle up with Melanie, later."

The silver BMW shot along the street as the mobsters watched the activities, laughing in jest. Candace was guiding the whip. Claire looked up from checking the bags of money and jewels.

"Let's head to the warehouse and get some stuff packed," Claire said.

They raced along the highway back to the warehouse and began loading weapon into the car. They packed an arsenal.

"Be careful. That C4 is right next to the cash and jewelry. Take all that we can carry. We might not be able to come back here for awhile," Claire shouted.

Both girls hurriedly packed Gucci duffels with cash and jewelry.

"No matter how this turns out, we need a vacation," Claire said. A half smile clung to her lips.

They loaded the 740IL and Candace jumped into the driver's seat.

"That bitch Melanie didn't put enough gas in the ride."

"Are we gonna need some?" Claire asked.

"Yes, we're gonna have to stop..."

They were heading to the highway when they spotted a man selling fruits at a stand.

"Hey mister fruit-man, can you tell me where I can get some petrol?" Candace asked, coming to a stop next to the stand by the roadside.

"I've got oranges, mangoes, sugar-cane..."

"Gas, do know where we can get some?" Candace asked.

"Let's get a piece of fruit," Claire suggested. Obligingly, the fruit-man approached the car window.

"Oh, gas is straight ahead next to the stoplight on your right as you go downtown..."

"Thanks," Candace said.

"Do you have papayas?" Claire asked.

"You want papaya?" Candace asked, looking at her watch.

"Hell yeah, he's cute..."

"I said papaya, not papa," Candace said, shaking her head. The sisters laughed. "Get me one."

"Two pappies," Claire said, laughing.

The fruit-man gave the girls the fruit. As soon as they paid him, the police cruiser swung around. Candace gunned the engine of the BMW and the car took off with such great force, the fruit man had to hold on to his stand.

"Don't forget your change...!" he yelled just as the car whizzed by him.

CHAPTER 26

In New York, it was after three in the afternoon when Sean received the phone call he had been waiting for.

"Bitch," he uttered when he hung up.

She wanted him back. He smiled at the thought. She wanted to kiss and make up. Claire was begging for him to come back and fucked her. This was the moment he wanted to have the upper hand for once on the sisters. Sean immediately dialed his PO, who sounded really happy. He encouraged him to make the trip. Hours later Sean waited outside an airport in Miami.

"There he is signed, sealed and delivered."

Candace pointed when she spotted Sean with his bag slung over his shoulder. He was pacing back and forth.

Claire quickly guzzled liquor from a bottle. She poured the rest of the bottle out and smashed it on the street.

"Oh shit! What the fuck is up?" Sean shouted, jumping back out of the way of the flying glass.

"I was drinking, honey. I didn't understand until too late what was happening. Please get inside the car. Oh don't worry, Candace and I are gonna make it up to you. You can tell your man that you had both the Osorio sisters," Claire smiled.

He was about to answer but words failed him. Sean's brow furrowed as he stared in disbelief at Claire's flirtatious expression.

"And at the same time." She winked.

"That's a lie. He ain't getting none of me," Candace started.

"C'mon, play along, Candace," Claire whispered.

She turned to Sean and shimmied out of her dress. When Candace did the same, Sean raced inside the limo. In no time flat he was feeling on both sisters' breasts. He was beside himself. Candace did everything to keep herself from killing him right then and there. That was all Claire's plan. The chauffer glanced back at the girls in amazement but said nothing. He drove through the airport and headed back to the hotel.

"I expected you to rescue me from all those bad men, Sean," Claire said.

His ego was inflated as he relaxed between the two topless and gorgeous women. They passed a series of sports field.

"I'd love to have you in me right now," Claire said, eyeing Sean. She rubbed on her sister's crotch. Candace pulled Claire close and kissed her, thrusting her tongue deep into her sister's mouth.

Sean stared at the sisters making out. The sound of their lovemaking excited him. He tried to look at the dark outdoors. No matter what he did, he couldn't wipe the images from his mind. Trepidation mounted in his heart, but he wanted both the sisters. Tits and asses blurred his sight. The limo stopped and Sean and the sisters walked out.

Candace was stripped down to sheer panties. He felt excitement when he saw her shaven crotch. Claire held him by the waist. She undid his belt buckle. Sean drank lustily from a bottle of Bourbon. He shook off the anger he felt toward them and his dick began rising to the occasion. Finally he could tell everyone he banged the Osorio sisters. Candace, the teaser and Claire—nothing would be better to have them both at the same time. He gulped from the bottle.

"Sean, c'mon let's go do it outside under the moon," Claire suggested.

They led him to the middle of a soccer field. Sean drained the bottle of liquor and flung the empty bottle in the air, laughing eagerly.

"Yeah, yeah!" he yelled excitedly. "We gonna get it on and do some serious outdoor fucking and all that, baby. Tonight's the night..."

Claire kissed him and said, "Baby, let me help you out them jeans."

"I can't lie. That truth-serum I was drinking made me like that. I gotta confession..." he slurred.

"Yes, really...? What is it, Sean?" Claire asked, while unloosening his buckle.

"I've gotta tell you Claire. I always wanted to fuck you and Candy!" he shouted.

Claire pulled his jeans half-way down. All of a sudden Sean felt a kick in his crotch coming from behind.

"Bitch, I know you love that rough stuff, but what da fuck was that for?" he screamed, spinning around.

The motion caused him to lose control and he stumbled. Wobbled, Sean fell to his knees when Claire's right cross nearly knocked his block off.

"Hey what da fuck you doing, bitch?" he shouted angrily.

"No one call my sister Candy, but me, you fuck-face!"

The blow upside his head had him dazed and shaking his noggins vigorously, trying to regain his senses. Things only got fuzzier. This shouldn't be happening. His thoughts went haywire when Candace held her gun and she started cursing him.

"You fucking rat...!" Candace said. "You think I'd ever let your punk ass inside me?" Candace smacked him with her gun. His arms lashed out. "You touch me and I'll splatter your fucking shit for brains all over this field," she said, taking deadly aim at his dome.

"You see a man's face, but you don't see his heart..." Candace deadpanned.

He looked at Claire with pity and shame in his eyes. Her face was twisted with a frown of disappointment. She held her gun down and walked behind him. She took his wallet and removed the detective's card from it. Realizing his fate was gloomy, Sean knew that even begging probably wouldn't help, but he was reaching for straws.

"I know, I know, but I ain't really told them anything. Look you know that I don't know enough to say much about nothing..."

"Shaddafuckup you big bitch...!" Candace screamed in his face.

Sean could feel all her rage spewing spitballs on his confused face. The alcohol had left him woozy. He was shamefully on his knees with his jeans pulled down and preventing him from moving. Sean glanced up timidly at Candace's face, knotted in a scowl of no mercy. This was it. He wanted to save his hide, and started ratting. Now his doom was near.

"Why do you wanna kill me so badly...? I didn't mean to hurt you. I'll leave you and your sister alone and that'll be that. I won't go back to New York. I won't testify against y'all. Candace, let me live... Please! It was Jacque. It was his fault. He brought me into this! Please don't kill me!"

"I ain't gonna kill you, you piece of rat shit... No, I ain't gonna waste my bullets on your bitch-ass," Candace said, lowering her gun and walking away. For a second, Sean felt better. Then he heard, "But my sister will."

Sean look horrified and suddenly the darkness lit up. Phiz-zit, phiz-zit, phiz-zit—the muffled sound heralded the informer's execution. Three bullets hit Sean point blank. His body crumpled. Blood streamed onto the field. Candace kept walking, not looking back.

With tears streaming down her face, Claire bent over and was removing his wallet when she realized that Sean was still breathing. She used her hunting knife, deftly cutting his penis off and stuffing the bloody mess into his mouth. Gunshots pierced the night's air. Claire took the wallet and wiped bloodstains from her nude body on his jacket. She was still crying while walking away.

Hurrying to catch up to her sister, Claire saw Candace waiting for her. Together the scantily clad sisters walked hand in hand back to the waiting limo.

"What about your boyfriend?" the chauffer asked when they got inside.

The question lingered for a few seconds. Claire glanced at Candace, who was staring straight ahead.

"He had a sudden change of mind that was caused by a splitting headache." Claire said as she sat in the car. The chauffer closed the door and took his place.

"I don't think he ever really loved you anyway," Candace said.

"All this pain for a two-timing dick... Take us to the hotel, please," Claire said, sounding angry. The limo sped away.

CHAPTER 27

The next day, news of Sean's murder was all over the airwaves of Miami. Local television stations carried live updates about the grisly way Sean's body was found on the soccer field. His entire body was filled with bullet holes. His penis was cut off and stuffed into his mouth. Melanie held her cheeks in both hands watching the television report. She immediately dialed the Osorio sisters' hotel room.

"Hello, turn on the television? Why? My boy...? Oh, let me see what you're talking about."

Candace turned the television and watched intently. She saw the officers looking at a body covered in sheets.

"The Florida State police are asking anyone with information to call their hotline. As was earlier stated, information is sketchy at the moment, but suspects are being sought by the police in an execution

*style murder. The killing occurred last night in the Orange Bluff area...
The man, who has not yet been identified, was found with his pants down
with three bullets in his skull... The police have no leads..."*

"He got mad and left us last night. Wrong move... He shouldn't
have done that," Candace said. "The other job is a go... You too, bye..."

She hung up the phone and joined Claire in the shower.

"It's gotta be tonight. They found the rat's body. Dead in the
field like any rat should be."

Claire didn't answer. While water ran off her smooth skin, she
was wishing she could drown the whole incident. She knew nothing
could change their situation now except for them to leave the country
immediately. Otherwise the sisters would be facing all kinds of charges.
They took a long shower, dressed and packed. The sisters had to leave
in a hurry.

"Let' go out to the where the boats are by the warehouse. We
need a nice yacht heading for Cuba."

"Please Claire, I'd go to Cuba in a little bucket," Candace said.

In the parking lot, the sisters checked their weapons and money.
They wanted to get transportation and would have to pay. Candace got
behind the wheel and started driving to the docks on the outskirts. She
could see the heavy police presence along the way. Candace decided
to go through a police barrier. Immediately after crossing she realized
that the chase was on. Candace floored the accelerator and the BMW
ripped through the streets. She swung in and out of traffic and ran into
a problem when she saw a crew of street workers. Not slowing, she

drove straight for them and the crew parted.

"What da fuck...?" shouted a worker.

The police cruiser was flying through and other police cars joined in the pursuit.

"You got this?" Claire asked her sister.

"I'm born for this," Candace answered.

The BMW was flying like a bat out of hell. Candace deftly steered the ride around corner after corner with the police dogging their tail. With clever whip control, Candace was able to get the vehicle on to the highway. Quickly she got off in the meat packing district. They had run out of gas.

"Let's find someplace to lay low for a while," Claire suggested.

The sisters jumped out the car and retrieved all their bags. They ran through the warehouses and found an isolated office space.

Tony, Goldie and his gargantuan goon sat in the car. They had been tailing the sisters and now watched from a safe distance down the block. They watched the three bodies in body bags being rolled out.

"There's something fishy for you," Goldie said.

"What?"

"They didn't take that two-timing broad out..."

Claire had really given Melanie a knockout punch. It was meant only to dazed Melanie, but it did more. Melanie was rolled out on a stretcher. She appeared to be alive but hurt.

"How long am I gonna be in the hospital?" Melanie asked an EMS worker.

"We gotta take you to hospital fpr observation," he answered.

The undetected eyes continued to follow the progress of EMS workers and the police. They observed and waited from their car.

"That's just girl power. The moment I laid eyes on them two, I knew..."

"Now we'll really have to settle with that broad, boss."

"You're right. The enemy of my enemy is a friend of mine," Goldie said, looking at his watch. "It's still early in the game."

"They sure put a dent in the faggot's ass!"

"Well they saved us from doing that faggot."

"Ha, ha, ha," they laughed, watching everything.

CHAPTER 28

Sirens blared and helicopters hovered outside. The warehouse where the Osorio sisters were holed up in was quickly being surrounded by the authorities. Everyone was there— the Miami Dade county police, the state police and members of the special task force. Claire and Candace peered out the window and examined their chances for a getaway. The authorities were crawling all over, along with squads of SWAT people and tactical personnel.

"I must admit, we've had a nice run for what's that worth," Candace said.

"It ain't over. It's not over just yet," Claire said, breaking the glass. "Fuck all y'all!" she screamed, firing shots from two automatic weapons.

"You know we didn't actually say goodbye to Mimmy."

"This is a shoot out, sis. It certainly doesn't mean goodbye," Claire shouted, letting off shots from a M16.

The officers immediately took cover and returned fire. Explosions occurred when machinery were hit by heavy artillery. Flying bullets broke glass and destroyed equipment, but the sisters were unscathed. They heard the blaring sounds of the authorities.

"Give up. You're surrounded. You cannot escape."

"Your jails will never see us," Candace screamed as she fired.

The sisters were aware that they would not be able to sustain the kind of firepower required to hold off forces of this magnitude. They sat down together to plan another avenue of escape. A fusillade of bullets came through the window and Claire hit the deck hard. It was apparent that they were in a deathtrap.

"Are you alright, sis?" Candace asked. There was no immediate response. "Claire? Talk to me."

A few anxious seconds elapsed before Claire spoke.

"That shit was real close. My ears are still ringing."

"What're they shooting at us with?"

"I don't know. We're not gonna be able to match them."

"Yeah, I hear you."

"Look at this," Claire said, struggling to her feet and pointing to a hidden trap-door in the floor.

"What is this place, some kind of storage?" Candace asked. Then she crawled over to the door.

Candace cleaned it off and tried raising it. "Shit, this is heavy."

Both sisters struggled with the door. They finally managed to lift it open. They peered in.

"It's some kind of a tunnel or sump'n."

"Where do you think it leads to?"

"I don't know, but I'm telling you, I'm willing to find out," Claire said.

"Did you bring the C4?"

"Yep, just in case," Candace said.

"Why don't you slap it on this trap door and let's see where this leads to."

"Once that shit goes off, this door will be sealed."

"No kidding. We'll be through this door with no reentry," Claire said.

The barricade set up by the police now expanded around the entire circumference of the place. There were no longer any exchanges of firing. A car pulled up and a beautiful detective walked out. Although it was getting dark, she wore sunglasses. Lt. Cooksey escorted Street to the communication hub.

"Boys, this is Officer Street, one of ours," Lt. James Cooksey said. "The FBI guys want to be in charge out here."

The lieutenant walked to where the federal agent stood waiting.

"Street was living with the sisters when she was a youngster back in New York. In the time she left, they've made quite a name for themselves, but this is where we will tear that name right down,"

Cooksey said with confidence.

A federal officer took Street by the arm and spoke to her.

"So how long have you been working with the Miami PD?"

"I've been here in Dade County nearly a year and a half..."

"What you did you do before that?"

"I was in college and..."

"College...?"

"Yes college, and after I got my associates I joined up and now I'm two years away from my law degree."

"Sounds like you're smart and made nice career choices."

"I did, but I need to graduate then pass the bar..."

"What are you waiting for? Why haven't you graduated yet?"

"Time... The higher in rank you go, the less time you have to do other things but work and I've been promoted so many times, I ran outta time."

"Decisions..."

"This assignment... The case of the two girls you lived with. Could be a major conflict huh?"

"Yes, maybe, but I'm an officer."

"Why did you accept the assignment?"

"I thought I could help..."

"And I understand you had a recent run-in meeting with them. What was their frame of mind?"

Street thought about it for a beat. She wanted to open up and reveal exactly what she observed. The sisters seeming enjoyment of the violence, like it was a game they were playing. She kept her mouth shut because she didn't know what Claire and Candace would do to win.

"They may listen to me. Please give me another shot," she pleaded.

"We've got them pinned down in there. You could talk to them if you want. I got the tactical teams on standby. They're trapped on the first floor. We've got people searching to get us a copy of the floor plan of the building. We've sealed the entire area off. There are no avenues of escape. As soon as we get the plan sent to us, our tactical people will study it before we move in..."

"May I make a suggestion?" Street asked.

"Sure, I'll entertain anything right now."

"I think I know both sisters well. I'm very familiar with them."

"Okay, we'll try anything. Whatever you know that can be used to capture them and save lives, we'll be more than willing to try another way.

"Call off the guns, the snipers... Lemme go in there and talk to them..."

"Like you did before, Street...?

The chief of the federal agent and Street both turned to see that the voice belonged to Lt. Cooksey. He waited for an answer, but Street was surprised. There was no answer.

"I tried to bring the fugitives in without violence. There's nothing wrong with that," Street said.

"But that could be very dangerous. They're armed and have

been shooting to kill."

"I know, but I'm willing to give it another try."

"You'll be endangering your life and we cannot provide any type of cover to ensure your safety," Cooksey said, moving in closer. "I'm in charge and we've got them covered, so we'll wait them out."

"But—"

"But nothing... If they don't surrender in another thirty minutes, then we're going in, tear gas and all..."

"Well you can give me that time to try and..."

"It's out of the question, Street."

Sheryl Street smirked in disappointment and turned as if she was about to walk away. Then she caught herself and faced the federal agent chief who had been listening to the verbal exchange.

"Please give me a shot at it, sir."

"You're attending law school, you have your life to live, why would you want to risk that for these killers?" the chief asked. .

The question rang out in the silence. Sheryl Street thought for a while before she answered.

"I'm their adopted sister," she finally answered in relief. "Will you let me talk to them?"

Lt. Cooksey looked at the Street as if she had just grown two horns. The chief nodded to him and Cooksey scratched his head in frustration, turned and shouted into a microphone hanging around his neck.

"All right, everyone stand down. No one is to fire a single

shot," he ordered. He turned to Street and spoke. "Okay Officer Street, proceed. I hope you know what you're doing."

"Thank you," Street said, walking forward.

"Thank me? Oh no, Street. Thank your friend in the Feds. You've got exactly five minutes to make something happen. Then we're going after them with SWAT. Take this. It's live," Cooksey said and handed Street a mega-phone.

Detective Street walked slowly to the warehouse. She put the megaphone to her lips and cleared her throat. Then she began to speak.

"Candace, Claire, this is Officer Street. The Miami police have the whole place completely surrounded. Please, you can both make this a better situation if you both surrender. Throw out your weapons and come out with your hands up. There is no way either of you are gonna escape. Please give up."

There was silence. Street turned around and shook her head. She saw the artillery assembled and how Cooksey licked his lips in anticipation.

"Okay ladies, I'm gonna come inside," Street said.

Street handed the mega-phone back to Cooksey and moved forward to the entrance of the warehouse. She released her service piece and let it fall to the ground.

"What the hell! Are you stupid or something?" Cooksey called out.

"They won't kill me. I got something in common with them,"

Street, cautiously making her way inside the warehouse.

Claire and Candace were watching the detective's activities from the window. They looked at each other as Street came to the entrance.

"I'm unarmed," Street said, walking inside. She stood for a beat at the doorway as if expecting someone to invite her all the way in. "Please don't shoot. I just wanna talk to you both."

Street walked inside the opened warehouse and stood in the middle of the floor.

"See. I'm unarmed," she said waving her arms in the air. "No weapons..."

"That's your stupidity," Claire fired back.

"Don't shoot! Please," the detective said.

"Stand right there where we can see you and don't try any funny shit. I swear I'll blast your ass," Claire threatened.

"You've got two minutes," Candace showed herself and the detective walked over. She could see both sisters now.

"Nobody's gonna blame you for walking out. You're gonna be chatted up at water coolers all over the country. You don't have to end it by being slaughtered."

"It's obvious you haven't been doing your homework, dick," Candace countered.

"Why?"

"Never again will anyone look down on us. That's what this is about, dignity and respect," Claire said, smiling.

"Do what we want, when we want to. The Osorio sisters live by their own rules. Nobody tells us what to do."

Street listened to the words rolling easily off Candace's tongue. She was convinced they weren't afraid of dying. Sheryl reached for her calling card.

"Mimmy loves her two beautiful girls who are her daughters. I know you love her also. She sends her regards. You've made your reputation on the streets, now give up and live for her at least."

"Is that it? Then you've delivered your message. Mimmy's a good woman," Candace said holding two guns at ready.

"Pat yourself on the back on your way out," Claire said, gripping an Uzi.

"Detective, don't you ever come back around us. And you better let Mimmy know that we kept our promise. You can go now, Detective Street," Candace said, raising her weapons.

"I guess there's no turning back for you... I mean you could still save your own lives... They are willing to make a deal. You won't do too much time. Don't make a negative situation worse by—"

"Detective, we're through talking. Your time's up," she said, cocking the gun and raising the loaded weapon to Street's chest.

The detective turned and walked out of the warehouse. Candace aimed at her head but didn't pull the trigger. Street continued outside to where the squads of police waited impatiently to mount a major assault on the Osorio sisters. News cameras and reporters swarmed the area, ravenously seeking the story. They clamored to Detective Street as she made her way back to safety.

"What's it like in there?"

"Are the sisters gonna give up?"

Uniformed police desperately tried to hold back the wave of reporters.

"How's it inside there?" Cooksey asked and the detective shook her head. "That grave, huh?"

Cooksey signaled to his units. They converged on him.

"All right, this is it. I want the tactical guys in there. Eliminate and return."

Claire let off an outburst of automatic weapon fire.

"Everyone git down," Cooksey screamed.

She smiled when they all scrambled for cover. It was the same power she felt when she was in the park years ago. She never wanted to give up that power again. The squads opened fire and the loud sounds of explosion crashed the temporary uneasy cease-fire. Squads of trained police teams moved in on the warehouse, firing powerful caliber weapons. The resulting explosions spread around the girls like wildfire. The sun was beginning to set.

"A fine pickle we're in, sis," Candace said, loading her weapons.

"Are you giving me the sad song?" Claire asked with sarcasm.

Claire looked on as Candace clutched the weapons.

"How is it?" she asked.

"We're running out of ammo," Candace answered.

"I hear you, sis," Claire said.

"I'd be damn if I'm gonna be cooped up in anybody's prison," Candace said.

"Me too, sis, me too," Claire agreed.

"I'm not afraid as long as you're with me, Claire. I know Mimmy will be sad that we went out like this," Candace said.

"People got to do what they got to if they want to make it. There are no right or wrong ways, sis," Claire said.

"Oh man, what a nice day to go out," Candace said.

"It's time," Claire said, looking at the trap door.

Candace scurried over to it and attached the explosive device to the latch on the door. She grabbed an M203 and fired a grenade, which landed in the center of the squads moving forward. They quickly fell back, ducking behind cover, and returned fire. Bullets crashed through the warehouse with deadly accuracy. One hit the explosive device on the lock. There was a major explosion. Flames and debris were hurled everywhere.

"Take cover, take cover!" the squad leaders sounded off.

There were simultaneous explosions. The situation was being closely followed by the news as well as a black sedan parked a little away from the scene.

"If those two were in there, then they gotta be deep sixed now. C'mon, let's get the fuck outta here."

"Ya right. Nobody, not even my girls could've survived that. Shame, shame, shame, they had so much talent, them two." Melanie pulled out a handkerchief and swabbed her eyes.

"Hey Goldie, let's go find us a spot with some nice peppers and sausage."

"That's a good idea. Pauli, get me the fuck outta here."

"I know the perfect spot," Melanie said.

They drove off as the tactical teams rushed into the demolished warehouse and began searching through the rubble.

"I'm sorry, there's no one in there," the lieutenant said.

"They deserve whatever they got," Cooksey said triumphantly.

Street sat on the hood of the cruiser and whispered a silent prayer for the two sisters. She shook her head when she saw the level of destruction.

Blinded by the explosion, Street and the other officers were totally unaware that the collapsed warehouse led to a tunnel on the other side of the street. The Osorios crawled from underneath the rubble and climbed up the manhole. They peeked left and right before walking up a short ramp and into the sewage canals. The sisters emerged underneath a Mall in downtown Miami. Their tattered clothes and messy appearances were eyesores, but they were happy to be alive. Despite the upturned noses of the downtown shoppers greeting them, the sisters laughed and skipped joyfully away.

CHAPTER 29

The next day, the Miami police led by Lt. Cooksey and Street, who was operating on a tip from Jacque, busted into a large storage warehouse rented by the Osorio sisters. The police had searched for the bodies and couldn't find any evidence of the sisters. It was as if they had vanished into thin air. No corpses, no ashes, no remains were found. The incident had the police baffled and searching for answers. Police however, did find the location of the storage used by the sisters.

The entire unit was filled with racks of new clothing from all the major stores and designers. Thousands of shoes boxes were found stacked neatly. A glass case filled with top shelf watches from Rolexes to Movados. There were thirty large televisions, DVD players, laptops, video game players, and Xboxes accompanied an assortment of electronic devices.

"These girls boosted and bought a whole warehouse of shit on stolen credit cards!" Lt. Cooksey said when he saw the sisters' bounty.

"Yeah, they won't be big pimpin' anymore," an officer joked.

"Goddamn!" the lead officer yelled. "No way are we gonna spend a whole month sorting through all this stuff. This is where the feds come," Lt. Cooksey laughed.

He got on the horn to the chief of the federal agents as his officers wandered through the place in jaw dropping awe.

"The Osorio sisters were no joke. Too bad they're not gonna need all these items anymore."

"You'd think those two girls were some kind of rich aristocrats, renting a damn storage filled with millions of dollars worth of stolen items."

"Yeah, they tried to be rich but sometimes things don't work out the way you plan," an officer said.

"You gotta plan to be around in the end, that's all."

The officers all laughed. They turned their attention to tagging the items and moving them out of the warehouse storage one at a time. There was a whole bunch of boxes of everything that didn't add up to much for the Osorio sisters.

CHAPTER 30

When Sheryl pulled up and parked she could see all the cars. Most of the mourners were still at Mimmy's apartment. As she walked in, everyone was eating and drinking heartily. Mimmy hobbled around making sure everyone had eaten. Then she sat in her chair in the living room and coldly stared when Sheryl Street approached.

Others recognized her and the tension in the room hit the ceiling. Melanie and a crony jumped in her path, but Mimmy waved the angry Latina off.

"Let her come close." The grieving woman's voice trembled with anger.

Sheryl Street had waited long enough and walked directly to Mimmy. She pulled up a chair next to her and took a deep breath before speaking.

"I'm so sorry..." she started and broke down crying.

"You were doing your job," Mimmy said, touching her hand.

After a few minutes, she gave Sheryl a glass of water. On this early fall day when the leaves had changed, they spoke and wept together. Jacque was the first to come by.

"Hi Sheryl," Jacque said, interrupting the impromptu meeting between Mimmy and Sheryl.

"You're not to be blamed solely, Sheryl. We all should've helped their spoilt asses."

Mimmy shook head and anguish clouded the frown on her brows. "I wouldn't have all that tomfoolery. Maybe I was too protective of them," Mimmy mused. "Get her something to eat, Jacque," Mimmy said graciously.

Sheryl and Jacque walked away, hand in hand. Jacque led her out the now crowded living room. Settling for an almost private hallway, Jacque and Sheryl hugged for a beat. It was the first sign of sincerity that Sheryl had experienced since her return.

"Somebody is looking real good," Jacque smiled when they were alone in hallway.

"Hey Jacque, thanks," Sheryl said, embracing Jacque again.

"You know these people in the Heights don't forgive so easily. But they'll get over it."

"I'm not worried about anyone, but Mimmy. She's been through a lot," Sheryl said. "There's nothing else I could've done, but I feel like there was so much more that I could've done, Jacque," she continued.

"Trust me when I tell you she didn't really know them like I do," Sheryl said.

"She knew them. Mimmy just loved them too much to care about what they were doing. Mimmy thought they were actresses doing a movie in Cali until you blew them up."

"I know she really had no way of knowing. They were out in L.A. alright but it wasn't doing movies."

"Yeah, you know I knew the deal. I knew the real deal on that," Jacque said, reminiscing. "I remember too well when I went out there and visited them."

Candace was sitting in the bathtub while Claire gently applied soap to her naked back. Suds dripped down her honey shade depositing in the softness of her crevice. She was back working on perfect breasts. Two pairs of nipples, hardening to the touch like ripened fruits. Candace did likewise, a sensual bath for her sister. The sisters served each other with loyalty. Applying makeup to each other, they chose dresses for each other. Adoration was mutual, admiring in a huge mirror showering each other with compliments.

"Why Miss Candace, you look sumptuous."

"Why thank you Miss Claire. I'd say you're looking ravishing."

Playfully laughing at beauty, their tone changed to a more serious one. They continued admiring each other in another set of mirrors.

"Really though, the world isn't ready for this," Claire said, smacking her sister's sexy derrière.

"On that note, let's go," Candace said.

Grabbing Luis Vuitton handbags, they would go racing out the door. Their red Ferrari was downstairs in the parking lot. With Candace at the wheel, they speed away.

"Alright, strap yourself in, big sis. Rodeo Drive, here comes the Osorio sisters."

Summer sales always attracted shoppers. At Wilshire and Rodeo, they slowed, Gucci frames shielding their eyes, they looked for parking. Stores were receiving fall merchandise and were busy. The strip was always crowded. The sales staffs and security were running around, trying to meet the demand. The girls drove north on Wilshire and covered Rodeo.

Well-dressed and beautiful, the sisters were part of the young sexy women walking the streets. Their long legs attracted a fair share of attention on Daytona. They investigated the boutiques and went into Robinson's on the west. The girls went through Amelia Gray's before hitting Saks on the east corner.

All the high-end boutiques were their playground. Quickly they went through the sales racks, avoiding the salesgirls. Sweeping through Polo, carefully inspecting every piece of merchandise they lifted. Their game was boosting and they played it well.

"The sales staff is really busy," Claire noted, walked out of a store.

"It's too crowded for me to operate like I want to, big sis."

"Let's head over to Saks, Candy," Claire suggested.

"I want Gucci today..." Candace answered.

"When we're finished, Gucci will still be here. I promise you, Candy."

After exiting Saks with shopping bags, Candace and Claire strode into the Gucci store.

"Good day ladies, may I be of some assistance?" a salesgirl greeted.

"No thanks you," Claire responded.

"Very well... Enjoy."

"Thanks," Candace smiled.

Browsing, they spotted BCBG outlet. The girls hurried inside and went straight to the rack of leather pants.

"Candace, check out these riding pants," Claire exclaimed.

"I want to see the shoes," Candace said.

"We can see that on our way out," Claire said, examining the leather pants.

All items had security locks individually attached, but the sisters were not deterred, they were just scouting for cameras.

"This leather is really hot," Claire said.

"Yes," Candace nonchalantly replied.

"Let's go to the shoe department," Claire said, shaking her head.

Candace followed, wearing a smirk.

The doormen greeted them with a big smile and tilted his hat, helping them with the door, items on their shopping lists, slipped easily by security. Their arms filled with the days' bounty, they made their way out of store after store. Everyone treated them well.

"Let's put these in the car and have lunch," Claire said.

They strutted back to the car. Candace and Claire shared lunch outside at the Santa Barbara Biltmore. A glass screen door shielded them from direct wind off the Pacific coast.

"What would we be doing if we weren't doing this?" Claire asked between sips of sherry.

"We'd be busy playing with the law in New York," Candace chuckled, toying with the rare sirloin in front of her.

"You're getting much too sentimental for my taste. Let's just pay the tab and go," Claire said.

Candace boosted an expensive bottle of perfume while Claire distracted the salesgirls. Not to be outdone, Claire stole an expensive bottle of men's cologne from Elizabeth Arden store. During the transaction at the cash register, Candace paid for a small bottle of cologne and Claire stole a couple more bottles of fragrances. The girls regularly returned to the scene of their crimes.

"Will that be all today, Miss?" the salesclerk asked, ringing up and packing items in a bag.

The Osorio sisters walked out the store and into their Ferrari. Along the way, they spotted the Prada store.

"Oh don't tell me you're gonna stop in there? We've been in there too many times already," Claire said.

"You know, a girl can't have too many," Candace winked and smiled.

They both hurried inside and loitered, touching the merchandise. Their chic look amazed one of the salesgirls.

"I'm sorry to intrude but I couldn't help but ask. Are you two sisters? I know I've seen your faces before. At a modeling affair, maybe...?"

"Could be," Claire responded off handily.

"I know," the salesgirl smiled. "I'll keep your secret."

She was impressed and left Candace and Claire with a shopping bag and carte blanche to take as many items as they wanted into the dressing room.

Once inside, the Osorios worked as a team, moving rapidly but disciplined and deliberately. Claire took care of the security tags from all the items except one. They removed their clothing and cut the clothing label. Using a Sharpie, they marked the items as if they were defected.

Claire and Candace slipped into the new garments, placing their own clothing in the bags, with the unaltered items on top. The beautiful duo exited the dressing room and them by showing them some new suits. They ignored the sales person attempts to engage them. The sisters were gone before the sales person realized what was going on. Before the day was over, they would hit several more stores that evening, including Giorgio's and Versace. They stole several thousand dollars of merchandise and then went to the car as dusk drew near.

"I think the stores have seen enough of us for one day," Claire said. It was officially time to end the boosting spree.

"You think?" Candace chimed in and jumped into the driver's seat. Buckled up safely, they peeled away in laughter.

The sisters relaxed inside their Beverly Hills apartment, Candace poured gin and tonic for herself and Claire.

"Make mine on the rocks," Claire said.

Candace gulped the drink down. She mixed another while Claire slipped out of her clothes and busied herself going through the bags. She found a short mini skirt and put it against her hips.

"These will fit me nicely."

"I think they're too short," Candace said, handing her another drink.

Claire strutted around the apartment buck naked as if she was on a runway. Then she changed outfits and sashayed through the place.

"Smile for the cameras..." Candace laughed, drinking. "Damn you're the best booster. I still wanna know how you get the locks off?"

"That's for me to know and you to find out. I know we didn't get caught," Claire laughed.

"One day, I'm gonna find out," Candace answered with a wink.

She picked out a see-through, silk blouse and put in on. Her hands were massaging her perfect breasts while she stared in the mirror.

"I'll wear this without a bra," she smiled devilishly.

Claire drank before both sisters fell back in the plush leather sofa, laughing and toasting.

"This is the life," Claire said raising her glass.

"To the life... Ah the bliss," Candace said, smiling.

They finished drinking and unpacked the rest of the day's bounty. Carefully packing their closet filled with clothes.

"I can't believe that store wanted that much for this jacket," Claire said.

"Four thousand dollars, big sis... Whew," Candace whistled.

"That's simply insane, Candy..."

"Claire, you're not trying to answer my question, huh big sis?"

"What was that, Candy? I forgot?" Claire asked.

"Removing the sensors... Okay, you did it in Gucci and Giorgio's today. Last week when were in Theodore's. You did it a couple of times last week too. Please stop frontin' on your sis. C'mon Claire you know we always share and share alike," Candace said.

"I done told you Candy, if I tell you I gotta kill you," Claire laughed, staring at the overcrowded closet.

"We're running outta space, right?"

"Yeah, let's do what we always do and donate some of these clothes to the Salvation Army," Claire suggested.

"Okay, we can do that tomorrow. Right now I wanna hear some music," Candace said.

The exclusive surround sound of a Nakamichi stereo, with built-in wall speakers, hummed a song familiar to both girls. The Osorio sisters sang along with Jay-Z and Pharrell's Change Clothes.

Cause the proof is back just go through my rap/ New York New York yeah where my troopers at/ Where my hustlers where my boosters at/ I don't care what you do for stacks/ I know the world glued you back to the wall/ You gotta brawl to that/

Reminiscing brought back anxiety that Jacque couldn't deny. He was beginning to show his feelings when he spoke to Street.

"Mimmy always thought that they were fashion models and that's how they were making their bread. She didn't know anything else, until you and your cop friends blew them the fuck outta that meat warehouse in Miami," Jacque said. "If I knew that was how it was gonna end, Sheryl, I wouldn't have helped you."

Street could hear the sadness mixed with his frustration. Jacque couldn't hide his emotions and tears streamed down his cheeks. She reached out to hug him, this time he pushed her away. The sound of clearing throat was heard. Jacque and Sheryl turned to see Melanie. She put a cigarette to her lips and her crony rushed to light it.

"Melanie, how nice of you to join us," Jacque deadpanned, wiping tears from his face.

"She wouldn't have known anything and would've been spared

the embarrassment of knowing her two lovely daughters were murdered by a person who should be looking out for them. A person she took in and showed love to when she was homeless. Come see me when ya get back to Florida. I got some people who will be happy to meet ya."

"C'mon Melanie, it's not Sheryl's fault, they were boosting and were on the run after the killing out in..."

"Oh yeah...? And their father wasn't around—" Melanie started but Jacque quickly interrupted.

"Their father was molesting Candace and Mimmy kicked him out. Could it be his fault too?" Jacque asked.

"They started their life of crime on their own. Nobody forced them to do it," Sheryl said.

"Nothing was proven in a court of law, Jacque."

"They never gave the law a chance," Sheryl said.

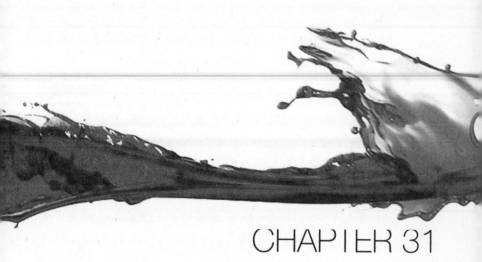

CHAPTER 31

A couple of weeks later in Miami, Melanie sat at a table in her Bar and Grill. A bottle of cognac and a glass still half filled sat on the table in front of her. A folded newspaper was also on the table. A handful of patrons sat in the sparsely crowded place.

Across the street from the parking lot, Claire and Candace Osorio sat disguised as men. They readied their weapons and were about to walk across the street to Mel's Bar and Grill.

The girls saw both Pauli and Goldie walking with bulges under their jackets. They were heading inside the same spot. The sisters stopped and lit a cigarette as both Pauli and Goldie whisked by them.

"Let them go right ahead," Claire smiled, nodding to Candace.

"They musta been in a hurry, huh? They didn't even shoot us a look," Candace smiled.

"Well one thing's for sure, these disguises are working just fine,"

Claire said.

"Just you remember to make your voice a little bit deeper, like I'm doing," Candace said and choked on the cigarette.

"Steady yourself, little sister. We don't need to talk to no one. When we go up that club, we should just start shooting. Here finish this cigarette and let's go shoot up the place," Claire smiled.

"I so wanna let that bitch Melanie see my face when I shoot her fucking ass, for setting us up with the feds," Candace snarled.

The girls continued smoking outside the club long after Pauli and Goldie had walked inside the Bar and Grill. Inside, the atmosphere was light with a small lunch crowd and a couple of strippers. Three men sat at the small bar and three others sat in booths with girls entertaining them.

Melanie relaxed and dipped a taco in a bowl of jalapeño sauce. She was about to put the chip in her mouth when Goldie and his goon walked in. She quickly opened a Chloe silver reptile tote and released the safety off her gun. Cocked and ready, Melanie stood and welcomed the mobster.

"Goldie, I'm so glad to see ya," Melanie said throwing her arms around the big intimidating frame of the mobster.

"Hey bring glasses for our guests and more ice, please," she shouted and motioned for him to sit. "Goldie, please join me and have a drink," she said.

"I'll deal with this one alone," Goldie said, waving his goon off. The mob henchman went to the bar. He quickly became enchanted by the dancers performing on stage. A topless woman rushed over with two more glasses. She poured the drinks.

"Get some girls and entertain his friend over there at the bar," Melanie said and winked at the waitress.

They waited until the waitress was out of earshot before they spoke.

"What're we drinking to?" Goldie asked, raising his glass and throwing the liquor down his throat. The goon did so also. "Not bad. Let's have another," he said pouring.

They drank another two rounds before Melanie responded.

"I know you've got a lot of good news, huh, Goldie?" she asked.

"I know *you've* got good news," Goldie smiled.

"I didn't get a bigger territory on account of anyone's demise..." she started.

Goldie reached for the newspaper and opened the page to an article showing the drug dealer's death in the hotel. The story revealed the connection of the dealer to organized crime and related the death to the hit on Maurice Tines. The case was closed.

"What about this?" he asked, staring at Melanie. "Somebody's has got to pay. He was carrying my money and my coke."

"How can ya be sure I was involved in...this?" she asked, throwing the newspaper down. Goldie watched as the pages fell out. The faces of the Osorio sisters were on an exposed page, a caption written below their mugs. Goldie picked up the paper and read a few lines. He threw the newspaper on the table next to Melanie's

"It just so happens that I now own the judge who gave you the information. I put two and two together and remember that you said the Osorio sisters were working for you. So I did some more poking around. Do you want me to continue?" he asked, pouring another round.

"Well you shouldn't go poking around so much. You liable to find things you don't want to," Melanie said, gulping the drink.

"Such as how you were using all the information the judge gave you to carve out your own little empire..."

"C'mon Goldie, ya can't possibly be holding anything against me. The Osorio sisters waltzed right passed ya and drove away with over a million in diamonds after they hit Mo and me. How do we get it back after the police put an end to their run? And I mean no thanks to ya! So, we all made mistakes, Goldie my love. Ya were supposed to get the ice off two broads and did ya? No. Do I run arguing with ya? No."

Goldie gulped another shot. His eyes wandered around the club and then settled on the two dancers doing a slow gyration center stage.

"He was corrupt and a faggot and we all hated him but somebody's gotta pay for the death of Mo Tines. Besides being a loud-mouth, sonofabitch, he was a made man. To off a made man, well ah... That indeed cannot go unpunished."

"Well, honey the Osorio sisters, they got their punishment already. And it was at the hands of the law. So that should be that." Melanie swallowed her liquor and poured another for herself and

Goldie.

"Any woman who would set up her fiancée is not worth her salt," Goldie said, watching a dancer's legs now spread as she slid up and down a pole. "When we first met, you were just like her," he said and drank.

"Yeah, but I fell in love with the right man, didn't I Goldie?"

"You were young and poor. You came from New York and had no one else to run to. I bought you a condo. I gave you credit cards. I even gave you your own business and now you're no longer pure. Money has spoilt you. It's made you greedy."

"It was my greed that made me build this place to what it is. See, now it's a first class joint. Take a look around ya Goldie. Me-Me Sunshine danced her ass and built this by her own sweat," Melanie said, beating her chest. "It was my legs that ache from dancing, and these men they came out to see my ass. My ass... Night after night... I did my part, Goldie. I did my part. I finished the job just like we all wanted."

"Then there was absolutely no reason for you to be making plans behind my back. The judge you're milking, I own him. The first thing I hear is that you're making secret deals, ripping off drug dealers who are carrying my shit. My shit!" Goldie shouted and slammed the glass so hard, the table rattled.

"Slow down, baby, before ya blow a valve," Melanie coldly said.

"If its one thing you should remember it's this; never steal from family, they know all your dirty secrets."

"Goldie, I had no idea that it was yours. Ya know I wouldn't... It was those greedy Osorio sisters."

Melanie started to speak but swallowed hard when she saw Goldie eyes twitching. She put her hand in the bag and deftly coiled her index finger around the trigger.

"At this moment it seems neither of us likes each other very much," Melanie said, looking in Goldie eyes as she spoke. He stared her down, looking directly in her brown eyes.

"You're right on that account." He poured two drinks and handed her one.

"What are we gonna do about this situation, Goldie?" Melanie asked, sipping.

"Unfortunately for you, Melanie, I'm in a position to enforce my dislikes." He pulled out a forty-five and put it down on the table as he spoke.

"I see what ya trying to say," Melanie said, calmly nodding her head.

"Yeah, you got it. Now, you have to pay. There's just no other way. You understand my position on this?"

"Goldie, I can't believe you're accusing me of doing anything wrong, when you know I've always done right by ya," Melanie pleaded, and coyly fixed the Chloe Tote with the gun centered on her target. "I had to sleep with that lil' dick-homo Mo Tines, and had to stomach him rubbing all over me, just so you could inherit all that was his. And now ya do this? Ya come to me with all this hate in your talk. I don't care if ya kill me. I did what I had to do, but I always loved ya... It was always Goldie."

Melanie spoke while sliding her purse towards Goldie chest. He was moved by her act and he relaxed his fingers. The gun sat on the table pointed at her. Goldie poured two glasses of liquor. His goon sitting at the bar was totally distracted by the dancers rubbing his dick and plying him with liquor. With this wave of pussy-popping strippers parading around him, he was in no position to see what was happening with his boss.

There was a loud bang. Goldie smiled then slumped over the table. Pandemonium broke and patrons ran screaming. Melanie tried to get away from the scene as quickly as possible. Pauli pulled out a razor and slashed her throat as she tried to run by him. Melanie kept running a few more steps and collapsed center stage. Blood oozed from her neck and mouth. Melanie legs kicked and her body was in the throes of death's dance.

Pauli walked over to where Goldie was slumped and checked him. He had cashed in. There was no breathing. People were running everywhere, leaving the scene. Amidst the chaos, Pauli quickly made his way out of the strip club. He didn't see Claire and Candace in their disguise waiting for him.

"Here he comes. Remember, just start shooting," Claire ordered.

"Allow me," Candace said. She immediately raised her automatic weapon, pumping off two rounds into Pauli. He froze, grabbing his bleeding stomach. There was a look of surprise on his face. "You're a bastard, Pauli. You cheated me out of killing my double crossing lover," Candace said, firing again.

Candace pulled the mustache from her lips and threw it at her fallen victim's face.

"You always hate mustaches, huh?" Claire said.

"I hated him more for killing my girl," Candace said.

"C'mon get over it, Candace. There'll always be others."

"Yeah, you're right, but Melanie was special."

"Aw, let's head down to Mexico. I'll find you some replacements."

Fifteen minutes later, the police arrived, swarming the scene. Detective Street strutted into the strip club. She looked at the body of Goldie slumped over at the table and made a few notes. Street walked over to the stage and saw Melanie's body. She looked at her face and saw the creepy, cold smile hanging from her lipstick-stained lips.

"Well, what're you looking at her like that for? She probably deserved it," Street shouted to a uniformed officer.

"Yes, you're right lieutenant," an officer said to her.

"Lt. Street, there's another body in the parking lot. I think you should come and take a look at it."

Sheryl Street walked outside to the parking lot and immediately saw the body of Pauli lying cold, bleeding.

"Is he alive?" Street asked the uniformed officer.

"No, he's had it, lieutenant. But his fake mustache was lying next to his body. It's as if the killer ripped it from off his face."

The officer put his gloves on and picked up the fake mustache. He stashed it into an evidence bag and handed it to Street. She examined it carefully.

"Hmm... Why would his mustache be ripped from his face?" Street asked aloud.

"I really don't have any clue except he grabbed it off in an act of frustration."

"Or maybe his killer or killers just don't like mustaches. No..."

Lieutenant Street handed the plastic bag containing the evidence back to the uniformed officer and walked away, shaking her head. She headed back inside the club. Just before going inside, Street smiled, still shaking her head.

Epilogue

Sheryl Street, dressed in civilian clothes, walked to the entrance of the mental institution on her way to visit her mother. This time, she told herself, she would go completely through with the visit. She had with her a Barbie doll and sugarless candy. Sheryl straightened the collar of her pastel colored blouse and walked into the center. Dr. Katz smiled when she came inside.

"I'm glad you've decided to come back and visit," the doctor said.

"It's been sixteen years. I'll be visiting my mother regularly," Street said with a soft smile.

Claire and Candace sat eating in a parked Chevy truck. They had ditched the guns and the male costumes. They were ghost to everyone but themselves. The sisters ate and drank then smoked a cigarette in silence before Claire spoke.

"You know I really feel like going to Mexico, but I feel we got some unfinished biz to take care of in New York. Do you know what I mean, Candy?"

It seemed like minutes passed and Candace had said nothing. She continued eating her Subway sandwich and staring from out the truck's window. Candace turned to see her sister starting the truck and then turning it around, heading in the other direction.

"Why do you wanna go back to New York now, big sis?"

"I gotta settle with Jacque for selling us out.

You know that, Candy," Claire answered.

"Is that all there is to that, big sis?"

"Revenge is a dish best served cold. And oh, you know, Candy, I will not lose..."

She turned on the radio and the cab of the truck was filled with the sound of Donna Summer track. The engine hummed and the sisters sang along to the disco classic.

> *Hey... toot, toot...*
> *Ah... beep, beep...*
> *Toot, toot...*
> *Ah beep, beep...*

"Beware the fury of a patient man"
—Dryden, *Absalom and Achitophel*

Thank you to the Augustus Manuscript Team— the dream team, Robert Guinsler, Clarence Haynes, Jason Claiborne, Tamiko Maldonado, Juliet White, Anthony Whyte. Thanks for a job well done.

WHERE HIP-HOP LITERATURE BEGINS...

AUGUSTUS PUBLISHING

Augustus Publishing was created to unify minds with entertaining, hard-hitting tales from a hood near you. Hip Hop literature interprets contemporary times and connects to readers through shared language, culture and artistic expression. From street tales and erotica to coming-of age sagas, our stories are endearing, filled with drama, imagination and laced with a Hip Hop steez

on the streets of New York only one color matters...

HARDWHITE

BASED ON THE SCREENPLAY BY NATIONAL BESTSELLING AUTHOR

SHANNON HOLMES

Novel by
ANTHONY
WHYTE

Hard White: On the street of New York only on color matters
Novel By Anthony Whyte Based on the screenplay by Shannon Holmes

...re pitch black...A different shade of darkness has drifted to the North Bronx
...as Edenwald. Sleepless nights, there is no escaping dishonesty, disrespect,
...stility, treachery, violence, karma... Hard White metered out to the residents
...cious have big dreams but must overcome much in order to manifest theirs.
... story of triumph and tribulations of two people's journey to make it despit
...ama you won't ever forget...Once you pick it up you can't put it down. Deftly
...e based on the screenplay by Shannon Holmes, the story comes at you fas
...sight to what it takes to get off the streets. It shows a woman's unWlimited l
...s is a rider and will do it all again for her man, Melquan... His love for the s
...vered. Her love for him will melt the coldest heart...Together their lives har
...e crucible of Hard White. Read the novel and see why they make the p...

When Love Turns To Hate

A NOVEL BY

SHARRON DOYLE

When Love Turns To Hate
By Sharron Doylee

...regulating from down south. He rides with a new ruthless partner, and they're...
...money. The partners mercilessly go after a shady associate who is caught in an...
...their road to riches. Petie and his two sons have grown apart. Renee, their m...
...decision when one of her sons wild-out. Desperately, she tries to keep her v...
...ile holding onto what's left of her family. Venus fights for life after suffering a br...
...hare goes to great lengths to make sure her best friend's attacker stays ruine...
...aining and teeming with betrayal, corruption, and murder, When Lo...
...ixed with romance gone awry. The drama will leave you panting fo...

Street Chic
By Anthony Whyte

A new case comes across the desk of detective Sheryl Street, from the Dade county larceny squad in Miami. Pursuing the investigation she discovers that it threatens to unfold some details of her life she thought was left buried in the Washington Heights area of New York City. Her duties as detective pits her against a family that had emotionally destabilized her. Street ran away from a world she wanted nothing to do with. The murder of a friend brings her back as law and order. Surely as night time follows daylight, Street's forced into a resolve she cannot walk away from. Loyalty is tested when a deadly choice has to be made. When you read this dark and twisted novel you'll find out if allegiance to her family wins

SMUT central
By Brandon McCalla

Markus Johnson, so mysterious he barely knows who he is. An infant left at the doorstep of an orphanage. After fleeing his refuge, he was taken in by a couple with a perverse appetite for sexual indiscretions, only to become a star in the porn industry... Dr. Nancy Adler, a shrink who gained a peculiar patient, unlike any she has ever encountered. A young African American man who faints upon sight of a woman he has never met, having flashbacks of a past he never knew existed. A past that contradicts the few things he knows about himself... Sex and lust tangled in a web so disgustingly tantalizing and demented. Something evil, something demonic... Something beyond the far reaches of a porn stars mind, peculiar to a well established shrink, leaving an old NYPD detective on the verge of solving a case that has been a dead end for years... all triggered by desires for a mysterious woman...

$14.95 // 9780982541586

Dead And Stinkin'
By Stephen Hewett

Stephen Hewett Collection brings you love as crime. Timeless folklores of adventure, heroes and heroines suffering for love. Can deep unconditional love overcome any obstacles? What is ghetto love? One time loyal friends turned merciless enemies. Humorous and powerful Dead and Stinkin' is tragic and twisted folktales from author Stephen Hewett. The Stephen Hewett Collection comes alive with 3 intensely gripping short stories of undying love, coupled with modern day lies, deceit and treachery.

$14.95 // 9780982541555

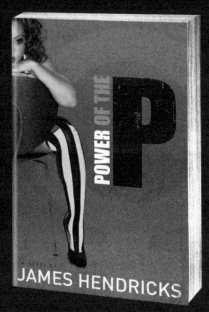

Power of the P
By James Hendricks

Erotica at its gritty best, Power of the P is the seductive story of an entrepreneur who wields his powerful status in unimaginable — and sometimes unethical — ways. This exotic ride through the underworld of sex and prostitution in the hood explores how sex is leveraged to gain advantage over friends and rivals alike, and how sometimes the white collar world and the streets aren't as different as we thought they were.

$14.95 / / 9780982541579

America's Soul
By Erick S Gray

Soul has just finished his 18-month sentence for a parole violation. Still in love with his son's mother, America, he wants nothing more than for them to become a family and move on from his past. But while Soul was in prison, America's music career started blowing up and she became entangled in a rocky relationship with a new man, Kendall. Kendall is determined to keep his woman by his side, and America finds herself caught in a tug of war between the two men. Soul turns his attention to battling the street life that landed him in jail — setting up a drug program to rid the community of its tortuous meth problem — but will Soul's efforts cross his former best friend, the murderous drug kingpin Omega?

$14.95 / / 9780982541548

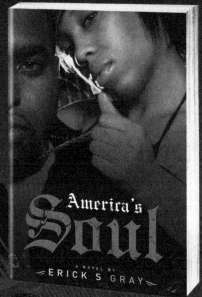

GHETTO GIRLS IV

Young Luv

ESSENCE BESTSELLING AUTHOR
ANTHONY WHYTE

Ghetto Girls IV Young Luv
$14.95 // 9780979281662

Ghetto Girls
$14.95 // 0975945319

Ghetto Girls Too
$14.95 // 0975945300

Ghetto Girls 3 Soo Ho
$14.95 // 0975945351

THE BEST OF THE STREET CHRONICLES TODAY, THE **GHETTO GIRLS SERIES** IS A WONDERFULLY HYPNOTIC ADVENTURE THAT DELVES INTO THE CONVOLUTED MINDS OF CRIMINALS AND THE DARK WORLD OF POLICE CORRUPTION. YET, THERE IS SOMETHING THRILLING AND SURPRISINGLY TENDER ABOUT THIS ONGOING YOUNG-ADULT SAGA FILLED WITH MAD FLAVA.

Love and a Gangsta
author // **ERICK S GRAY**

This explosive sequel to **Crave All Lose All**. Soul and America were together ten years 'til Soul's incarceration for drugs. Faithfully, she waited four years for his return. Once home they find life ain't so easy anymore. America believes in holding her man down and expects Soul to be as committed. His lust for fast money rears its ugly head at the same time America's music career takes off. From shootouts, to hustling and thugging life, Soul and his man, Omega, have done it. Omega is on the come-up in the drug-game of South Jamaica, Queens. Using ties to a Mexican drug cartel, Omega has Queens in his grip. His older brother, Rahmel, was Soul's cellmate in an upstate prison. Rahmel, a man of God, tries to counsel Soul. Omega introduces New York to crystal meth. Misery loves company and on the road to the riches and spoils of the game, Omega wants the only man he can trust, Soul, with him. Love between Soul and America is tested by an unforgivable greed that leads quickly to deception and murder.

$14.95 // 9780979281648

The lights went out and the mayhem began.

It's gritty in the city but hotter in Brooklyn where a small community in east Flatbush must come to grips with its greatest threat, self-destruction. August 14 and 15, 2003, the eastern section of the United States is crippled by a major shortage of electrical power, the worst in US history. Blackout, the spellbinding novel is based on the epic motion picture, directed by Jerry Lamothe. A thoroughly riveting story with delectable details of families caught in a harsh 48 hours of random violent acts, exploding in deadly conflict. There's a message in everything… even the bullet. The author vividly places characters on the stage of life and like pieces on a chessboard, expertly moves them to a tumultuous end. Voila! Checkmate, a literary triumph. Blackout is a masterpiece. This heart-stopping, page-turning drama is moving fast. Blackout is destined to become an American classic.

BASED ON SCREENPLAY BY JERRY LaMOTHE

Inspired by true events

US $14.95 CAN $20.95
ISBN 978-0-9820653-0-3

CASWELL
COMMUNICATIONS

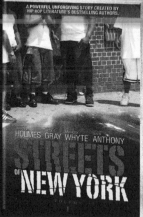

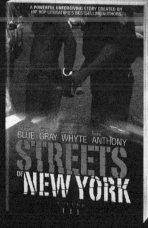
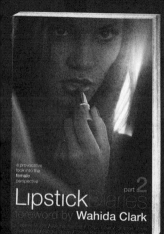

What's in a Word?

A Dictionary of Daffy Definitions

Rosalie Moscovitch

Illustrated by Andy Myer

Houghton Mifflin Company   Boston   1985

Library of Congress Cataloging in Publication Data

Moscovitch, Rosalie.
    What's in a word?

    Summary: Offers unusual definitions using puns
and illustrations including "Finite: Lovely evening" and
"Beriberi: A double funeral."
    1. American wit and humor. 2. Wit and humor,
Juvenile. [1. Wit and humor. 2. Puns and punning]
I. Myer, Andy, ill. II. Title.
PN6163.M64   1985   818'.5402   85-5174
ISBN 0-395-38922-4

Printed in the United States of America

V   10   9   8   7   6   5   4   3   2   1

Dedicated with special affection to a certain Cheshire Cat in brown cords.

—*R. M.*

To Mom—who loved her puns almost as much as her son.

—*A. M.*

Foreword

What's in a word? You'd be surprised! There's often more to a word or phrase than initially meets the eye — or ear — and you may see or hear something unexpected. That's what happened to me, and that's how I gradually discovered hundreds of ordinary words and phrases that now have very different meanings, many of which you'll find collected here.

This little book is for fun and for sharing with others who enjoy a good groan. I hope you enjoy it as much as I enjoyed creating and compiling it. But be careful: you may become addicted to this kind of word–twisting and come up with a few "daffies" of your own!

—Rosalie Moscovitch

What's in a Word?

A

Abyssinia: *So long!*

Accommodating:

Acrostic: *An angry little parasite.*

Affable:

Ancipital: *. . . which is why I'll never share my milkshake with Ann again.*

Anther: *Rethponth to the quethtion.*

Anticlimax:

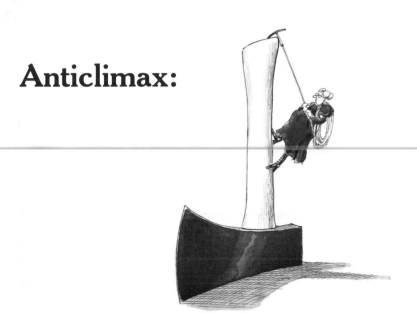

Antonym:

Apéritifs: *Two holdup men.*

Archaic: *What we can't have and eat it, too.*

5

B

Balsam: *Cry a little.*

Banquet: *It rained on the Savings and Loan.*

Benign: *What eight will do if you add one more.*

Beriberi: *A double funeral.*

Bobby sox: *Blows struck by a British policeman.*

Bonaparte:

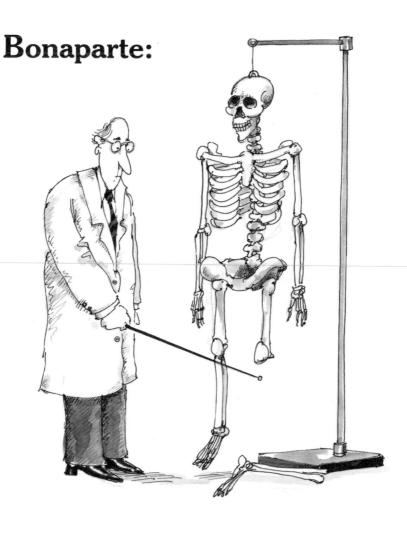

Buckshot: *Another dollar wasted.*

Bulletin: *The gun is loaded.*

Bulwark:

C

Cabinet:

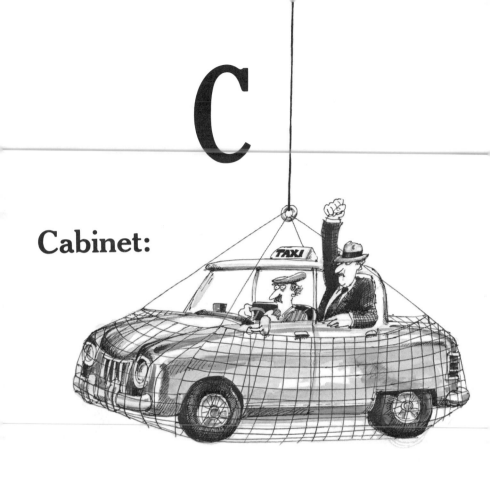

Caesar: *Grab that woman!*

Camelot: *Where used desert animals are sold.*

Candies:

Cantaloupe: *They forgot the ladder.*

Cantankerous: *Our captain can't stop the boat from drifting away.*

Castanet: *Go fishing.*

Catsup:

Cauterize: *What Pa did when he flirted with Ma.*

Champagne: *Artificial window glass.*

11

Classic: *All the students are ill.*

Combat: *Very relaxed flying mammal.*

Condescending: *The prisoner is going downstairs.*

Coward: *Moo!*

Curtail: *The part of a mutt that wags.*

D

Dead Sea:

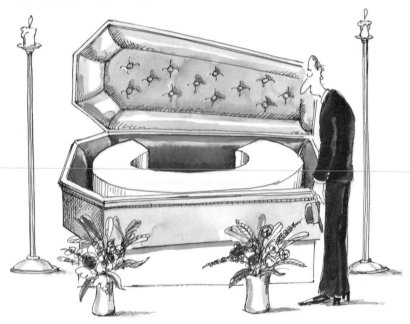

Debate: *What goes on de end of de fishing rod.*

Deceitful: *There's no room to sit down.*

Deduce: *It follows de ace.*

Deliberate: *What a messenger must do with a telegram.*

Denial: *Egypt's river.*

Dialogue:

Dilate: *Live to a ripe old age.*

Directorship: *The Princess of Wales did a terrible steering job at sea.*

Disdain: *The Viking right here beside me.*

Dogma:

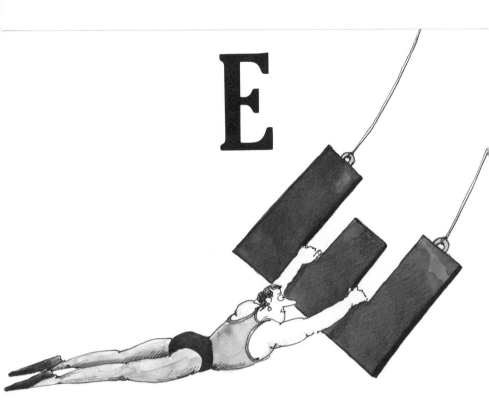

E

"He flies through the air with the greatest of ease."

Eclipse: *What the barber does.*

Elapse: *How a dog drinks his water.*

Enterprise:

Entity: *N, O, P, Q, R, S, T.*

Erasing:

Escalator: *...if she's too busy to answer you now.*

Ethereal: *Rithe Krithpies, for instance.*

Euthanasia: *Teenagers in Mongolia, China, etc.*

F

Felonies: *Prepared to pray.*

Finite: *Lovely evening.*

Flippancy:

Forborne:

Formaldehyde: *What the outside skins of cows do.*

Fulgent: *A man who has eaten all he can.*

Furlong: *That dog needs a haircut.*

G

Gallup poll:

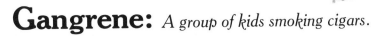

Gangrene: *A group of kids smoking cigars.*

Gangway: *Many people on the scale at one time.*

Germinate: *Two quartets from Berlin.*

Gladiator:

Gruesome: *A little taller than before.*

H

Hemlock:

Hierarch:

Hirsute: *What the sloppy dinner guest spilled soup on.*

Histology:

Hominy: *What amount?*

Homogeneous: *Einstein's residence, for instance.*

I

Ideal: *My turn to hand out the cards.*

Implies: *The little devil is not telling the truth.*

Income tax:

Infantry:

Infer: *How Eskimos are dressed.*

Innuendo: *Where you might keep some of your plants.*

Instinct: *What happened after the skunk wandered into the little hotel.*

Intense: *Where Indians sometimes lived.*

J

Jacket: *What you do to your car before changing a flat tire.*

Jacquard: *It follows the ten in a deck.*

Jargon:

K

Kidnap:

Kindred spirits: *My relatives absolutely detest alcoholic beverages.*

Kiwi: *That door opener is really tiny!*

L

Laccolite: *Be in the dark.*

Lactic: *The clock isn't working.*

Lambaste: *Marinade for shish kebab.*

Laminate:

Lawsuit:

Literate: *What some thoughtless people do to a highway.*

Livelihood: *Very frisky criminal.*

M

Malign: *What I wish the fish would bite.*

Maximum: *A very fat mother.*

Metaphor:

Miasma: *What's making it difficult for me to breathe.*

Migraine: *These oats belong to me.*

Minimum: *A Maximum who dieted successfully.*

Misinform: *Young woman in good shape.*

Mistletoe:

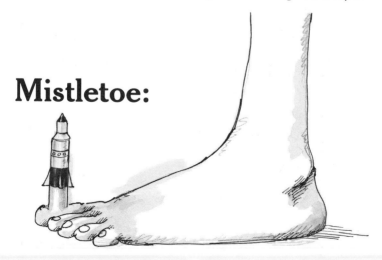

Moralize: *Additional forces from friendly countries.*

Mutilate: *What alley cats do.*

Mysticize:

N

Nitrate: *Sir Lancelot's fee for services.*

Nomad:

O

Offense:

Orienteering: *A piece of jewelry from China.*

Ottoman: *Car dealer.*

P

Pacifier: *Give me a light, please.*

Paradise: *You need this in Monopoly and other games.*

Parasite: *The Eiffel Tower, for example.*

Pastilles: *Dad's a shoplifter.*

Pectose:

Perverse: *Poetry by a very contented cat.*

Polytechnical: *The parrot stole five cents.*

Populate:

Portend: *The last drop of wine in the bottle.*

Prestidigitate:

Prophecy: *University lecturer on a cruise.*

R

Ransom: *Jogged a little.*

Razorbill: *What the doctor had to do when she didn't pay the first time.*

Rehearse: *Furnish the mortuary with a new limousine.*

Rodent: *A crack in the highway.*

Rugby: *An insect found in carpeting.*

Russian dressing:

S

Scold: *I'm freezing!*

Shamrock: *Fake diamond.*

Sign on the dotted line:

Silicone:

Sorbonne:

Soupçon: *Come and get it!*

Strew: *That's a fact!*

Subdue: *The Nautilus should arrive any minute now.*

Surveys:

Swiss fondue: *There's a pregnant deer in the Alps.*

T

Tangent: *Sunburned fellow.*

Tapestries: *What the owner of sugar maples does each spring.*

Tectonic: *Swallow medicine.*

Tenantry: *Thirteen.*

Theodicy: *One of Homer's epics.*

Tolerant:

Toupee: *The hardest part about a bill.*

Toxophily: *Speaks very badly.*

Tyrannize:

V

Vanity: *Truckload of orange pekoe.*

Versifier:

Vertigo: *What I don't know whenever vacation time comes around.*

Viper: *It cleans your vindshield.*

Vitamin: *What to do if a guest appears at your door.*

W

Weedy: *A very small letter.*

Well bred:

Window: *Hit the jackpot.*

Z

Zeolite: *What one may do at the end of a tunnel.*

Zero: *The worst seats at the theater.*

Zulu: *Bathroom at the London animal park.*

But What Does It All Really Mean?

Abyssinia: *the former name of Ethiopia*
Accommodating: *obliging*
Acrostic: *a word puzzle in which certain
    letters (usually the first in each line)
    form names, titles, etc.*
Affable: *friendly, easy to talk to*
Ancipital: *two-edged*
Anther: *the part of a flower that makes
    and holds pollen*
Anticlimax: *a disappointing conclusion*
Antonym: *a word having an opposite
    meaning to another word*
Apéritifs: *appetizers*
Archaic: *ancient*

Balsam: *a type of evergreen*
Banquet: *a feast*
Benign: *benevolent, kindly*
Beriberi: *a disease caused by a
    vitamin deficiency*
Bobby sox: *ankle socks*
Bonaparte: *Napoleon's last name*
Buckshot: *large leaden shot for
    shotgun shells*
Bulletin: *a brief news statement*
Bulwark: *a defensive wall*

Cabinet: *a cupboard for displaying or
    keeping a collection*
Caesar: *the family name of the early
    Roman emperors*
Camelot: *where King Arthur had
    his court*
Candies: *sweets*
Cantaloupe: *a kind of melon*

Cantankerous: *cranky, ill-natured*
Castanet: *a rhythm instrument*
Catsup: *a sauce, usually made
    with tomatoes*
Cauterize: *to sear*
Champagne: *a sparkling white wine*
Classic: *an outstanding example
    of a type*
Combat: *fighting, battle*
Condescending: *patronizing*
Coward: *a person lacking courage*
Curtail: *shorten*

Dead Sea: *the salt lake between Jordan
    and Israel*
Debate: *discussion*
Deceitful: *dishonest*
Deduce: *conclude, reason*
Deliberate: *done on purpose*
Denial: *a refusal to admit the truth
    of a statement*
Dialogue: *a conversation between two or
    more people*
Dilate: *widen*
Directorship: *the position or office
    of director*
Disdain: *scorn*
Dogma: *authoritative teachings*

"He flies through the air with the greatest
of ease": *a line from the song "The
    Man on the Flying Trapeze," by
    George Leybourne*
Eclipse: *a cutting off, or dimming,
    of light*
Elapse: *to pass or slip away, as time*

Enterprise: *a daring project*
Entity: *a being*
Erasing: *rubbing out*
Escalator: *a moving stairway*
Ethereal: *delicate, spiritual*
Euthanasia: *mercy killing*

Felonies: *serious crimes*
Finite: *having a definite end*
Flippancy: *disrespectfulness*
Forborne: *refrained, held back*
Formaldehyde: *a preservative and disinfectant*
Fulgent: *shining*
Furlong: *a measure of length equaling ⅛ of a mile*

Gallup poll: *a public opinion poll*
Gangrene: *death or decay of a part of the body caused by lack of blood*
Gangway: *a passageway*
Germinate: *to start to grow*
Gladiator: *a person who fought in the arenas of ancient Rome*
Gruesome: *horrible and repulsive*

Hemlock: *a poisonous plant*
Hierarch: *the chief of a sacred order; high priest*
Hirsute: *hairy*
Histology: *the study of animal and plant tissues*
Hominy: *coarse corn meal*
Homogeneous: *of the same kind*

Ideal: *perfect*
Implies: *suggests*
Income tax: *a tax on the earnings of a person or business*

Infantry: *foot soldiers*
Infer: *to deduce*
Innuendo: *a hint, insinuation*
Instinct: *a natural aptitude*
Intense: *extreme, strong*

Jacket: *a short coat*
Jacquard: *fabric woven with an intricate pattern*
Jargon: *the technical language of a special group; lingo*

Kidnap: *to carry a person off*
Kindred spirits: *people who are attuned to one another's feelings*
Kiwi: *a flightless bird native to New Zealand*

Laccolite: *a mass of igneous rock intruded between layers of sedimentary rock*
Lactic: *pertaining to milk*
Lambaste: *to beat or scold severely*
Laminate: *overlay, cover with thin sheets*
Lawsuit: *a case before a court*
Literate: *able to read*
Livelihood: *means of earning a living*

Malign: *to slander*
Maximum: *the most*
Metaphor: *the use of a word or phrase to imply a comparison*
Miasma: *an unhealthy fog or atmosphere*
Migraine: *a type of headache*
Minimum: *the least*
Misinform: *to give wrong information*
Mistletoe: *a parasitic shrub*
Moralize: *to explain the moral meaning of a lesson*

53

Mutilate: *to deface or maim*
Mysticize: *to make mystical*

Nitrate: *a chemical compound (NO₃)
made of nitrogen and oxygen*
Nomad: *a member of a wandering tribe*

Offense: *insult, transgression*
Orienteering: *a type of race, in which
participants have to make their way
across land they're unfamiliar with,
using just a map and a compass*
Ottoman: *a sofa or footstool*

Pacifier: *something that soothes or calms*
Paradise: *heaven*
Parasite: *something that lives off
something else*
Pastilles: *flavored or medicated lozenges*
Pectose: *protopectin (a pectic substance
found in plants)*
Perverse: *contrary*
Polytechnical: *a school offering
courses in many industrial arts and
applied sciences*
Populate: *to people, or provide with
inhabitants*
Portend: *foretell*
Prestidigitate: *to perform magic tricks*
Prophecy: *a prediction*

Ransom: *a payment demanded for the
return of a kidnapped person or
stolen property*
Razorbill: *a diving bird inhabiting the
Northern Atlantic*
Rehearse: *practice*
"Rhapsody in Blue": *a musical work by
George Gershwin*

Rodent: *a mammal of the* Rodentia
*order, such as a mouse, rat,
mole, etc.*
Rugby: *a kind of football game*
Russian dressing: *a type of
salad topping*

Scold: *berate*
Shamrock: *a type of clover*
Sign on the dotted line: *a direction given
on a form or contract*
Silicone: *a compound used in insulation,
coatings, paints, etc.*
Sorbonne: *a university in Paris*
Soupçon: *a very small bit*
Strew: *scatter*
Subdue: *tame, calm down*
Surveys: *detailed examinations*
Swiss fondue: *a dish made of cheese,
wine, etc., melted together*

Tangent: *touching at one point*
Tapestries: *woven rugs or wall hangings*
Tectonic: *pertaining to structure*
Tenantry: *tenants as a group*
Theodicy: *a work attempting to justify
the ways of God to man*
Tolerant: *permissive*
Toupee: *a small wig covering a bald spot*
Toxophily: *love of archery*
Tyrannize: *to oppress*

Vanity: *conceit, pride*
Versifier: *a poet*
Vertigo: *dizziness*
Viper: *a poisonous snake*
Vitamin: *a component of most foods,
necessary for proper nutrition*

54

Weedy: *full of weeds*
Well bred: *well brought up*
Window: *an opening in a wall*

Zeolite: *a mineral naturally occurring in lava cavities*
Zero: *nothing*
Zulu: *a member of a Bantu nation of southeastern Africa*